IS THERE A TRAITOR IN THE HOUSE?

A CRIME CLUB SELECTION

As a member of U. S. Intelligence's hush-hush Section Q, Selena Mead was on constant call. But the charming widow had no way of knowing the effect a party girl's near-fatal fall from a bridge would have on her immediate future.

Section Q was anxious to find if a connection existed between the "accident" and Congressman Jeff Stone—a man being considered for the Vice-Presidential nomination. So Selena was asked to get close to Stone, and find out how far his personal problems had driven him toward personal gain under the cover of his prominent position.

Scene: Washington, D. C.

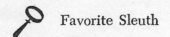 Favorite Sleuth

IS THERE A TRAITOR
IN THE HOUSE?

by *Patricia McGerr*

Published for the Crime Club by
Doubleday & Company, Inc., Garden City, New York
1964

Library of Congress Catalog Card Number 64–24530
Copyright © 1964 by Patricia McGerr
All Rights Reserved
Printed in the United States of America
First Edition

There is a city called Washington
There is a body composed of two houses
and known as the U. S. Congress
There are spies and counterspies
But the events chronicled in these pages
and the characters who take part in them
live only in the imaginations of author and readers

For Stewart Beach
to whose inspiration and guidance
Selena owes her existence

IS THERE A TRAITOR IN THE HOUSE?

CHAPTER ONE

Wednesday, March 11, 1964

8 A.M. "Ambassador Henry Cabot Lodge won a smashing victory in the New Hampshire primary. Running well ahead of Senator Goldwater and Governor Rockefeller, he achieved a write-in vote that . . ."

The clock radio switched on automatically and Selena heard the words through a veil of slumber. She was dreaming of Simon, a quiet simple dream of digging clams on the Maryland shore and roasting them by moonlight. She sank her face more deeply into the pillow as if to bury it in the sand and thus delay the moment of waking. It was half a year since her husband had been killed, but she still came to morning consciousness with reluctance and resurgent hope that she would find the dream real and reality the nightmare. She forced her eyelids open, tried to stifle the inner "no" that, less vehemently now, welled up against acceptance of his death, and faced another day.

While she dressed, the crisp voice told her of riots in Cambodia, demonstrations in Cyprus, the birth of an English prince, a filibuster in the Senate. National news flowed into local and she paused to hear the Washington weather. Mostly sunny, cold, a high near fifty degrees. A typical March day. She chose a white wool suit with huge black buttons and stepped into black pumps while the announcer told of an unidentified brunette found in critical condition under Calvert Bridge shortly after midnight. Made vulnerable to violence by the manner of Simon's death, she shivered slightly

14

and turned the knob to silence the description of the battered body.

An hour later she was in the Senate Press Gallery, where the talk was mainly of the New Hampshire voting and its probable effect on the Republican convention. She glanced over the releases the superintendent had put on the table along with yesterday's Congressional Record and picked out a statement by the chairman of a special House and Senate Joint Committee. It contained nothing that she didn't know already, so she folded it inward to use the back for notemaking.

"Executive session again today," a UPI man commented, noting her choice of material. "More expert witnesses from the Pentagon. And the data they're giving out is hot enough to dry up even my most dependable leaks. They not only won't talk facts and figures, they won't even drop me a hint as to the general over-all subject. Never have so many told so little to so few."

"Even the 'no comments' are off the record," a *Trib* man corroborated. "But that's not your problem, is it, Selena? Your magazine doesn't want the news till it cools off anyway."

"That's right," she agreed. "*Background* is willing to wait for you to ferret out the facts. Then we tell our readers what your stories mean. Actually, the only reason I'm interested in this release is because I'm lunching with the chairman and it seems tactful to be familiar with his latest quote."

"That will put you one up on him," the man from the *Times* assured her. "He's much too busy to read his own statements. But I'll be at the restaurant door waiting to interview you when you come out. Get a few words from him on what the Joint Committee's doing and you'll be the hottest news source on the Hill."

"The scoop may be his having apoplexy in the middle of his bean soup. My interview has nothing to do with his

15

committee. We'll be talking about the seniority system and how it works."

"Everybody knows it works fine," the AP man countered. "Assuming its purpose is to keep Congress from working."

From the gallery she went to the office of a congressman who was an outspoken critic of naming committee chairmen on the basis of length of service. So by the time she met her luncheon host she was well primed with arguments for him to answer. Normally a vigorous debater, he was today strangely subdued.

"You're tired," she said compassionately. "My deadline's a week away. Maybe you'd rather postpone our discussion till you're not working so hard."

"So you can mark me down as Exhibit A to prove that legislating is a young man's game?" He showed a flash of his usual spirit. "Not at all. Tiredness has nothing to do with it. It's just that I spent the morning listening to some pretty frightening statistics. In fact, if I were twenty years younger, they'd have scared me even more. But that's not in point. What else did that whippersnapper in the other chamber have to say about us dinosaurs?"

5 P.M. Her taxi turned into the narrow Georgetown street, let her out at her own front door. Going in, she felt again the flooding sense of emptiness. A surprising feeling, in a way, since she had, in the eight years of her marriage, grown used to entering an empty house, accepted the necessity of Simon's frequent absence. But in those days she had been anticipating, preparing for his return. To be expecting no one was to be truly alone.

To the right of the entrance was the den that had been Simon's office, her office now. In the sparse simplicity of its furnishings it held his presence more than any other room. His desk and typewriter, his files and books. Nothing changed, nothing missing but the well-broken-in pipe that had always rested in an ash tray near at hand. All this was now converted to her use, as she carried on the magazine job that had been his.

And for her use too was an invisible feature of the room, the soundproofing that Simon had installed when they first moved in. It no longer served the purpose he had announced for needing it—to protect his working quarters from the coming and going of her friends, the twitter of female voices, the rattle of teacups overhead. But the real purpose of its installation—the shutting off of voices inside the den from any outside ears—it served for Selena as it had for him.

She stopped by the desk only long enough to glance over the notes she'd made that day and drop them on the growing file. Then she shook off the room's many reminders and climbed the short flight of stairs to her living room. The house, she found, was not quite empty. Her maid, cleaning done and ready to leave, met her at the top of the stairs, stopped for a brief exchange on the day's activities. Her main news was that Selena's mother had come by with a new photograph of Selena's brother's children.

"She's bound that you'll come home to live again." Long service in the household gave her privilege as confidante. "This place and you all alone—" A wave of her hand took in house and garden, underscored the aloneness. "And now that your daddy's retired, how it would pleasure them to have you back. Why don't you think about it, Miss Selena?"

"I do think about it, Margaret," she answered. "But I'm going to stay right here."

She thought about it more as she relaxed in a warm tub, sloughing off in the gentle water the tension and tiredness of the day. It sounded so easy. To turn the clock back, wipe out the intervening years, be once again her parents' child. To ride to hounds, to follow the sun, to dance, to drink, to live idly and be gay. To go home again.

17

Yet this was, this roof in Georgetown, her first and only home. The rolling acres across the Potomac in Virginia, where her father had now settled to oversee his wide-flung business interests in what he called retirement. The house at Newport with its broad expanse of private beach. Both had been in the family for several generations, both were striking landmarks in her childhood memories. But in them Selena had always been a transient. Her most continuous recollections were of the stately but impersonal mansions in foreign lands where her father had been ambassador, where she had learned to speak three other languages before she'd been taught to read her own. And when her father had left diplomacy and returned permanently to America, it was time for Selena to go away to college. And Vassar had been more her home than the Virginia estate where, on vacation, she had been no less a visitor than the many guests with which the house had always overflowed.

On graduation she'd gone abroad to revisit the friends and scenes of her growing up. A final solitary pilgrimage before coming back for the autumn wedding that was to join her to the well-bred pleasant young man of whom her parents so thoroughly approved. It would have been, she realized, less a union of individuals than a linking of two names, two bloodlines, two fortunes. And in it she should have found an unexciting contentment. But at the end of that summer, one evening in Berlin, her path crossed Simon's. And for a few hours she was caught up in the danger that was, for him, a way of life. Caught up, never to break away.

So there was no VIP-studded wedding that fall, only a simple ceremony in a London chapel. If her parents were disappointed, they concealed it well, welcomed the young journalist as son-in-law, accepted uncomplainingly his refusal of her father's influence in finding a job that would bring greater prestige and income than the magazine whose high intellectual level kept its circulation low. There was, at least, compensation in the fact that his main base was Washington, that the house he bought made their daughter so accessible, still within the circle of their protection when her husband's work took him away. And since his death her mother had hammered on a single theme. Come home, stop brooding, let us cheer you, come back where you belong.

I'm not brooding, Selena told herself. She stepped from the tub, wrapped round a quiltlike towel. At least, no more than I would anywhere else. And this is where I belong. These were the walls that had encompassed, sheltered, all the years of her happiness. *J'y suis et j'y reste.*

She walked into the bedroom, turned the radio knob to get the half-hour news. But she was a few minutes late and the announcer had passed from national and international events to those of purely local import. He was talking about the girl under Calvert Bridge and Selena hurried to turn off the sound. She had no wish to hear of victims of despair.

8 P.M. Her dinner partner was a South American ambassador. The head of a giant corporation sat on her left. So alternate courses found her listening to flowery tributes in liquid Spanish and dire predictions of economic doom if the next election took the wrong turning.

"You write, then," said the former over the fruit in Kirsch, "for readers who are—what is this new word?—eggheads. That is the paradox of the United States. The most beautiful women must display their brains, while the clever ones bankrupt their husbands to achieve beauty."

Poking glumly at his trout, the tycoon also spoke of bankruptcy but on a more universal scale.

"Don't know what those voters in New Hampshire were thinking of," he grumbled. "Going for an internationalist like Lodge when they could have a genuine conservative. They're supposed to be hardheaded Yankees. If this keeps

19

up, we're headed for disaster. Your father will tell you the same thing. If we keep giving it away, we'll soon have nothing left."

She was glad when the arrival of the duckling let her turn once more to the predictable but almost sincere flattery of the diplomat. The occasion was a State Department dinner for the premier of a country in which Selena's father had once been chief of mission. In this company her magazine job was treated lightly as an amusing toy for a social butterfly, while her press colleagues looked enviously at her social contacts as an unparalleled tool for her trade. Of her third, and most important role, neither group was aware.

Midnight. She slid out of the Dior sheath, unbuckled the fragile sandals. The phone on her bedside table pealed sharply in the stillness. Two normal rings, one cut off at the first tinkle, then another full ring. — — · — International Morse code for the letter Q. She didn't touch the receiver but went to the closet and got out a sweater and skirt she could put on with speed. In minutes she was dressed again and waiting in her back garden for the sound of footsteps, human and canine, that would tell the other neighbors only that Hugh Pierce and Quorum were taking a walk. To Selena their approach—foreshadowed by the phone's coded summons—meant a new assignment for the top-secret branch of Security known as Section Q. She swung open the alley gate to let them in.

Hugh's crisp "Stay" to the great black Newfoundland was the only word spoken until they were in the soundproof den. Then the man from Q spread out a late edition of the afternoon paper which proclaimed in black capitals "PARTY GIRL IN SUICIDE LEAP" over a picture of a strikingly pretty girl with masses of black hair and large eyes.

"The girl who jumped off Calvert Bridge?" Selena asked. "Is she dead?"

"Not yet. But she didn't jump. Except for that, the story's accurate. Read it, then I'll fill you in on the rest."

Quickly she skimmed the paragraphs to learn that the girl's name was Gilly Conroy, she was twenty-eight, unmarried, winner of a string of local beauty contests in a southern state. She'd been in Washington for seven years, lived alone in a small apartment in an ultramodern building in the northwest section. She had no steady job but was well known on the convention and cocktail party circuit. Without being specific the story indicated that she lived well on irregular but liberal payments from lobbyists and salesmen. She was, for want of a more accurate and still printable phrase, a perennial hostess for organizations and companies that found her looks and other attractions of value in influencing legislation and the award of contracts. Found in early morning by a police car patrolling the Calvert Bridge area, she had been taken to a hospital where she lay in a coma. She had, it appeared, gone off one end of the bridge instead of the center. As a result, her fall had been broken by a tree and she'd landed on the earth bank instead of the pavement. Even so, the extent of her injuries gave her only an even chance to recover.

"If she's still unconscious," Selena asked, "how do you know she didn't jump? This story takes for granted it was attempted suicide."

"It's a natural conclusion," Hugh shrugged. "Most people found under that bridge are suicides. Usually successful. And in this case we've done our best to encourage that assumption. We're giving out a minimum of information, just enough to make it sound like a routine case and keep the press from blowing it up into a mystery. Whether the girl lives or dies, we want her marked off as one more illustration of the glamour-doesn't-buy-happiness text. So one piece of information that's strictly out of bounds is that the patrolmen came on the scene while she was still on the bridge. They were driving across Connecticut Avenue on Calvert when their headlights caught two figures—the girl and someone else, probably a man. They seemed to be struggling and as the patrol car speeded up, the man pushed the girl over the rail and ran off the other end of the bridge. By the time the cops got there he'd disappeared. That's a good area to vanish in, plenty of cover. They found the girl barely alive. That's how she's stayed ever since."

"And now Section Q has moved in," Selena said. "So it's more than just an ordinary murder. Was this—" She re-checked the newspaper for the name. "—Gilly Conroy involved with matters affecting national security?"

"She was—though we didn't know about it till today, and we still don't know how. Her name's not on any of our records."

"Then what brought you into it?"

"The police channeled it up the federal line as soon as they examined the body. They found a scrap of paper in her hand. They didn't know what it meant, but they could guess it had a TNT potential. It landed in our lap before she reached the hospital, so we were able to make sure the press got only the details we wanted them to have. And that doesn't include any suggestion of foul play. First, because we can't afford to arouse curiosity on the part of press and public and, second, because our chances of cracking the case are better if the other side thinks everybody's resting easy on the suicide theory."

"Are you going to tell me about the scrap of paper? Or does that fall into the category of things I don't need to know?"

"I'm going to tell you," he answered, "because it's where your assignment comes from. It was two scraps really, both small, the corner of an envelope and what it contained. Our conclusion is that they'd been fighting over it and the man pulled it out of her hand just before he knocked her over.

But she had her fingers clenched around a strip about an inch wide and three inches long. The particle from inside the envelope was covered with numbers—figures that would be meaningless to most people—but they check out as a time-table for troop landings in a Central Asiatic country in the event of a Red attack. Two days ago nobody had that data but three men in the Pentagon. Yesterday they were included in the hush-hush testimony given by one of those men at a closed session of a congressional committee. So it's a reason-able assumption that they were marked down by someone at the committee meeting and passed on to Gilly. Maybe she was supposed to give or sell them to the man who killed her, maybe not. That's a point we're not clear on. But one thing is certain. He got the rest of the paper that piece is ripped from and there's not much doubt it sets down specific plans from yesterday's testimony. That's information that could give the enemy a great advantage. So we're concentrating all our resources on finding the man who got the paper, as well as on locating and closing the leak from the Joint Com-mittee before even more dangerous facts seep out."

"But the Committee's still meeting. What about today's testimony? Aren't you afraid that will get out too?"

Hugh smiled faintly. "Today we were able to arrange a change of experts. Instead of hearing from the men who know our plans, they got estimates on enemy capabilities. If Peking wants those figures, they can be our guest. But we can't keep that going long. The rathole's got to be found and plugged fast."

"Have you any leads?"

"Yes, the scrap of envelope. That's what gave the police instant knowledge that this could be a delicate matter—and also gave us a head start on finding out what the figures meant and where they orginated. Because the piece in Gilly's hand was from an envelope's top right-hand corner. The spot where common folks put a stamp but where a congressman has his signature reproduced so his mail can go through without postage. All we had were two letters at the end of a name—"ne"—with an M.C. underneath to indicate a member of Congress. That narrowed us down to four whose names have that ending. We collected envelopes from their offices, compared the printed signatures. And then there was one. Representative Jeffrey R. Stone. Do you know him?"

"Not well. I've met him on the Hill, seen him at big receptions. It's barely a nodding acquaintance."

"By this time tomorrow," Hugh said, "I want you to be his closest friend."

Six months earlier she'd have argued, called the order impossible, absurd. But she'd learned the futility of argument and only said mildly, "You're asking for fast work."

"It's Stone I expect to work fast," he answered. "All you have to do is arrange to interview him for your magazine. No politician is ever too busy to meet the press. Set it up for late afternoon when it can spill over into cocktails and dinner. Then leave the rest to him."

"How easy," she scoffed. "You mean I just sit back and wait for him to tell me he's a spy?"

"Probably not," he returned. "Although I don't say it couldn't happen. Sex and sympathy make a powerful combination. In fact—" He tapped the newspaper photo. "That may be what got him into this mess. And if Gilly's the type that appeals to him, you've a head start. Because there's a remarkable resemblance."

Startled, she looked again at the picture, then back to Hugh. Realizing that he was anticipating an indignant protest, she bit back the words that rose to her lips, said nothing. His eyes showed amused awareness of her reaction.

"Oh, I know," he went on, "you wear different price tags. You're a true Virginia aristocrat and she's a small-town bathing beauty. Too much hair, too much make-up, too much sex projection. But cut away the brush and wash her face

and there's fine bone structure. And those great dark eyes—
well, since you don't care for the comparison, I won't go on
with it. Let's put it this way. If Stone is attracted by attractive women, he'll make the customary effort to know you
better. You reciprocate by learning all you can about him."

"You suspect him of passing information to the enemy?"

"At this point, we suspect everyone who had access to
those figures. Congressman Stone just happens to be the
only one whose name is directly linked with the passage.
And that proves nothing. Congressional stationery is easy
to come by. It could be purely accidental. That envelope
might simply have been a handy container for whoever jotted
down the notes. Or it could be an attempt to throw suspicion on him. You can be sure his isn't the only trail we're
following. We'll check out all the committee members, the
staff, the Pentagon team, everyone connected with that hearing. It has to be a crash program because every day that
passes makes it more likely the information will leave the
country. So while you're doing the personal bit with Stone,
there'll be some vast behind-the-scenes delving into his bank
account, his debts, his friends and foes, the skeletons in his
closet. Your part of it is to get inside his mind, find out what
makes him tick."

"Any specific questions?"

"Whatever you learn, tell us. Don't try to sift the evidence.
The most trivial-sounding fact might be pivotal. But what
we most need to know is motivation. Here's a man who's
shot up like a rocket and has a star-spangled future. Poverty
to prominence with all the Horatio Alger touches. He's
served four terms in the House and the polls give him a bet-
ter-than-even chance to move up to the Senate in the next
election. Unless he takes a higher leap."

"The Vice-Presidency, you mean. I've heard his name
mentioned in that connection. But you hear a new name
every day."

"That's true. At this point it's a horse race and all the horses are dark. But Stone's name is in the top six and it turns up on every list. He's a compelling speaker and those rackets hearings gave him nationwide TV exposure. So the chance is there."

"Then it seems to me," Selena said, "you've answered your own question. It's not credible that any man would jeopardize those hopes, that future. What could he possibly gain that would balance the risk?"

"There's a more ancient dialogue," Hugh returned, "that asks a similar question. What shall a man take in exchange for his soul? Now it's over to you. Tomorrow—or the next day—you may find a reason. Our job would be much simplified if we could write off every suspect who appeared above suspicion. But I've met too many spies who gambled large holdings for small stakes. Not political heights like this, but things of greater value. Like their honor, their liberty, their families' happiness. So we count out no one, no matter how unlikely. If you can gather information, or even an opinion, about Stone that will weight the scale in one direction or the other, it will speed up our investigation. And speed is our greatest necessity. Or rather, it's our second greatest. Number one is discretion."

"Section Q is always discreet."

"Right, but this time we must set new records. We're in delicate political waters and we have to pass through without raising a ripple. You can imagine the explosion if word gets out that we smell treason in one of the houses of Congress. And Stone's situation multiplies our problem. The slightest hint that he's under suspicion could eliminate his future. It might even become an issue in the national campaign and pull down his whole party in November. Or it might work the other way. He could be vindicated and made to appear the innocent victim of a witch hunt so he'd win a sweeping victory. From our standpoint, both results are bad. Section Q's existence and effectiveness depend on keeping our political chastity, doing nothing to help or harm either party or any candidate. If Stone is innocent, our checkup has to vanish without a trace. And if he's guilty—then I hope we can make him vanish."

"Oh!" She drew back a little from the implications of his words.

"This isn't a sporting event," he told her. "Here's a man who may be a traitor. If he isn't stopped, he may be Vice-President. And that job's only a bullet away from the White House."

"He can't be. He just can't. At least we assume he's innocent until he's proved guilty."

"In a law court, yes. But we're not administering justice, we're looking for truth. So we assume nothing. Start with an open mind, then open your eyes and your ears. Use whatever persuasion it takes to get him to talk and hope that he'll drop a clue."

"A clue," she said softly, "to what could lead a man to betray his country when it's given him so much."

"There are half a dozen standard motives," Hugh said. "One or more of them turn up in almost every case of treason."

"Money tops the list, I suppose."

"Yes, some sell, others buy. That's why we're going over Stone's finances with a microscope. Any sign of sudden wealth or, conversely, any desperate need for cash will be an alarm bell. But everything doesn't get on the books. So you watch too for indications that he's either improperly prosperous or close to bankruptcy. After money comes love—if you'll excuse the euphemism. We're tracing his connection with the Conroy girl, but you may be able to lop off some question marks in this area. How susceptible is he? Assuming she had him hooked, what would he give in exchange? To put it bluntly, would he pay off with American de-

27

fense secrets? Facts we can get. Dates and places we can run down. What we lack are the intangibles that feminine intuition can supply. While we research the women, we need a woman to research the man. And you're it."

"I see."

Their eyes met in eloquent silence. He was the first to turn away.

"I know how much I'm asking of you," he said. "Shall I wave a flag and make a Fourth of July oration to persuade you that it's vitally necessary?"

"No. You don't have to do that."

"Frankly, it's improbable that Gilly's charms alone would do the trick. The other, and more usual, side of that medal is blackmail. If they've been having an affair and the other group has evidence of it—well, at this stage in his career a little scandal could puncture some pretty big balloons. Again we come back to the question, what is Jeff Stone really like? How would he react to that kind of threat? Are his ambitions bigger than he is?"

"Could it be that he didn't need to be pressured, that he's actually a communist, believes in their system and wants to help them?"

"There's not a thing in his past pointing that way. In fact, everything he's said and done to date leaves an opposite impression. But a smart communist—and we give Stone full marks for shrewdness—would make that kind of record. So that's not ruled out either. It seems the only spy types we can't line him up with are the ones who do it for excitement, to break up their routine with adventure or make themselves important. Stone doesn't have to go out on a limb for kicks. He can get plenty fighting lions in the political arena."

"And from girls"—she glanced again at the newspaper—"like that."

"Perhaps. We're not sure yet how well they knew each other."

28

"But she ought to be able to explain everything—where she got the envelope, who took it from her—"

"When, what, why and how," he finished. "Yes, Gilly's the key to the whole puzzle and we've a long questionnaire for her. But we're pinning few hopes on getting it answered. The doctor says it's ten to one against her ever regaining consciousness. We purposely made the newspaper report a little more optimistic."

"Oh." Her eyes went back to the photo and the flamboyant beauty took on new pathos. "Then if she dies, you'll be looking for a murderer as well as a traitor."

"Yes. But I think when we find one, we'll have the other."

After Hugh left she remained for several minutes in the garden, remembering the time when she had believed that Simon had chosen this house for its combination of old-world charm and modern equipment, its special features of livability. She'd had no notion that its chief asset was its nearness to Hugh's house and the convenient alley connection or that the high brick walls separating their backyards from those of neighbors to the right, the left and across the way provided privacy of more than social value.

How often, in those days, Simon had left her in bed to go out for what he called "a last pipeful." She'd asked no questions then, kept herself from, even mentally, groping for explanation. She had not even let herself dwell on the coincidence of the abortive phone ringing that so often preceded his departure. Because of her presence, Simon made a pretext of answering the phone, put it down with a shrugged "wrong number." And she made a pretext of believing him, pushed away the picture of someone, somewhere, dialing their number, waiting through two full rings and cutting off the third at its beginning, then dialing again for one more uninterrupted ring.

The circumstances of their first meeting had made her aware that Simon's real work was counterespionage, his magazine job only a cover. And she could sense when he was on special assignment. But she had been told none of the details, had no knowledge of the peculiar significance of the signal "Q." What was not voiced did not have to be fully faced. And to what Simon did not want her to know she tried hard to close her mind.

She went back to the den, pulled out the blue-bound Congressional Directory, thumbed through the biographical section to Stone, J. R. His entry was one of the briefest in the book. Lack of ego, she wondered, or something to hide? Born in 1920. Graduated from his state university. Four years in the army. Law degree from Yale. Practiced law in his home town. Two years as city attorney. Elected to Congress in November 1956. Re-elected in 1958, 1960, and 1962. No mention of family.

Selena, jogging her memory, recalled talk of a separation or divorce. There was, she thought, something about a teen-age daughter and a battle over custody that had never reached the courts. In a town where gossip was a major industry, it was hard not to hear most of the private facts about public people. And a year ago Washington had been buzzing with innuendo about the Stones. But Selena instinctively turned from gossip, listened to such conversations with reluctance or not at all. She had tonight cause to regret that disinclination. More attention to what had been said then might be useful to her now. She put the book back on the shelf and went up to bed.

Sleep was a long time coming. This time, she thought mutinously, I should have made him get someone else. Another "party girl" like Gilly Conroy. Of all the jobs thrust on her by Section Q, none had filled her with such distaste. She thought back to the night, late last summer, when her comfortable, happy world had suddenly exploded. Hugh had come then to tell her that her husband was dead, killed by an enemy agent, and that his death must, for security reasons, be announced as accidental.

She had learned that night for the first time of the small special branch its members referred to as Section Q. Its operations could, when need arose, extend to all parts of the world, touch every field in which national security was threatened. It sometimes cooperated with, but was always apart from, all the other arms of intelligence. Yet its existence was known to only a necessary few, its agents were all anonymous, its successes were never credited. No one ever volunteered for its service; those few were tapped—as Simon had been—who could bring to it some specialty of nerve or talent, contacts or occupation.

Perhaps the most surprising revelation had been the emergence of Hugh Pierce as a leader in that inner circle. Selena had never suspected that the seemingly indolent artist who lived at the other end of the block was the man from whom Simon got his orders. Georgetowners saw him as a painter of modest talent and clownish exterior. Boyhood friends—like Selena's older brother who'd been at Harvard with him— deplored the fading of his once brilliant prospects. Only insiders knew him as a top operative for Section Q. Even now, seeing him in other company, she found it hard to reconcile his slouch and sleepy eyes, his lackadaisical attitude and general air of shabbiness with his flintlike alertness in private conference.

She had, in the first days of her widowhood, cooperated to solve her husband's murder and close the case on which he had been working. At its successful conclusion, Hugh had commended her as clever and courageous, then added, "In our organization we've a high degree of cleverness and an abundance of courage. But this job called for special qualities that only you could supply. There'll be other jobs like that."

They had come along often in those months, assignments for which Selena's background and talents, her family connections and circle of friends made her specially fitted. In the beginning she had tried to turn them down, to make him stop asking her, until at last Hugh said impatiently, "I know how you feel, Selena. You think that because Simon was killed on a job for Section Q, you want to have nothing to do with us. But the fact is, you believe the same things Simon did and you're not going to let his life go down the drain. Not as long as you're able to carry on. Willing or not, you can't say no to us. So why waste time arguing?"

She had, after that, kept her protests to herself, knowing that what he said was true. But it had not quenched the aversion with which she entered on each new task, her recoil from the deceit, the danger, the dirty underside of life which each revealed. And this one seemed now, in all its aspects, the most unsavory.

Yet even as she rebelled she knew she had no alternative. There was Jeff Stone who might be a traitor and might be Vice-President. And there was Gilly Conroy who was probably a harlot and possibly a spy but who did not belong, crumpled and broken, at the base of a bridge.

CHAPTER TWO

Thursday

Selena spent most of the morning on the phone. Her first call was to Congressman Stone's office to make the appointment which was as easy to get as Hugh had predicted. Then she talked in turn to a senator's wife, a political kingmaker, and a society columnist. To each, having covered the matters of mutual interest that served as pretext for her call, she dropped Stone's name and waited for reaction.

The wife, whose husband's name also turned up on lists of Vice-Presidential hopefuls, made a feeble effort at objectivity.

"So you're going to write about him," she said with envy. "He certainly has a genius for getting into print. Oh, I don't deny that he's hard-working and a very bright young man, but he has a shocking record of absenteeism for this session. They say he went way into debt in his last campaign and is desperately trying to earn enough for the next one. That's why he accepts all those speaking engagements. Besides the fees, they've won him a following in every section of the country. It gives him an unfair advantage over the men who stay here and do the grinding day-by-day work for which they were elected."

The politician was more blunt. "Interviewing Stone, eh, Selena. Watch out for a snow job. He's been all over the country trying to project the Kefauver image. A loner that nobody loves but the people. Successfully, too. Like him or not, if it looks like being a close election, we may have to give him second place on the ticket. He'll come on strong at the convention—as a favorite son-of-a-bitch."

But the columnist was congratulatory. "Nice work," she purred, "if you can turn it into play. And I'm sure Mr. Stone will see to that. This is a real tiger. So don't fight it, Selena. It may be your future."

"Heavens, Beebee, you do leap to conclusions." She forced herself to sound amused. "I'm only going to ask the man a few questions about the government."

"That's what Cleopatra said before she sailed up the Nile to meet Antony. Seriously, sweetie, you could do a lot worse. Jeff Stone is heading for high places. And you'd be a perfect team. The American voter likes a candidate's wife to be young and beautiful and with impeccable social status."

"There's also a preference," Selena suggested, "for one wife per candidate."

"True, but that's only for the top job and it will be a few years before our boy starts reaching for that. By then his divorce will be past history and the public won't be so prejudiced."

"Is he divorced now?"

"Not quite. There's a legal separation, but I understand he's put off final action till after the election. His reasons are partly financial. Partly because there's a fourteen-year-old girl neither wants the other to have. Mainly because it will mean laundering some very dirty linen in public."

"Really? What kind of dirt?"

"You do live in an ivory tower, Selena. A year ago people were talking of nothing else. Don't you remember Rachel Stone? A blowsy blonde. Well, I don't suppose she was blowsy when he married her and she probably wasn't a blonde either, but she got more so every year. I think she heard that Washington topped the nation for alcohol consumption and decided to do her patriotic bit to keep it that

35

way. She began making scenes at parties, calling him names, throwing glasses—very ugly. Once she passed out at a White House musicale, though of course they hushed it up as a fainting spell. They say their house was a shambles. Finally, he shipped the daughter off to boarding school and moved into a hotel. After that she left town."

"Poor man. How awful for him."

"Oh, it isn't all that one-sided. There are those who'll tell you he drove her to drink. When he had a home, he was seldom in it. Mostly he was out furthering his ambitions. But it's likely he was also finding entertainment along the way. A man like that doesn't have to look far. Talk about animal magnetism!"

"Are you just guessing?" Selena disliked the trend the conversation was taking but had to pursue it. "Or can you name names?"

"This is a very circumspect man. And he has two powerful reasons for keeping clear of scandal. He doesn't want to give his wife any counterevidence when the divorce comes up. And it might be death to his campaign. So all I have is some unsubstantiated rumors. One of them is rather interesting, though. It links him with the girl who tried to kill herself night before last. Gilly Conroy. You must have read about her."

"Yes, I—" She steadied her voice, tried not to show a quickening of interest. "I did see something in the paper. Were they—friends?"

"I can't prove it. And if he's as clever as I think he is, nobody can. But the ubiquitous 'they' say she used to wander in and out of his office rather freely. And the two of them have turned up occasionally in some of the offbeat night spots where they'd be least likely to be seen. And there are even those who claim to have seen him coming out of her apartment building at unusual hours. Maybe so, maybe not. It doesn't much matter now, since she's taken herself out of the picture. What else do you want to know about him?"

The question took her aback. "Why, nothing, I—"

A triumphant chuckle crackled along the line to her ear. "All business, is it, Selena? Just a few questions about government. This curiosity about his private life can't be all in the day's work—not for that thinking man's magazine you write for. Confess it, my dear, you've a personal interest. I not only don't blame you, I wish you luck. And when you've an announcement to make, I'd like it exclusive."

She entered Stone's suite at five-thirty. He was, his secretary explained, still on the floor of the House. He led her into the congressman's private office, gave her a mimeographed copy of his latest speech and left her to wait alone. Is this, she wondered, an opportunity of which I should somehow take advantage? She surveyed the room. A typical congressional office. A massive mahogany desk and swivel chair. Brass-studded leather chairs. Couch covered in dark blue leather. Filing cabinets and glass-enclosed bookcases built into the walls. A portable television set. A table littered with small articles manufactured in the congressman's district. The door through which she had come from the reception room. Two others which no doubt opened on to a bathroom and a coat closet. The desk, except for a neat stack of unsigned letters in the center, was a disorganized clutter of papers. Should she examine them, look for clues? She dismissed the thought as absurd. She'd find nothing but routine government business, probably suffer the supreme embarrassment of being caught in the act. In proof of her point, the secretary came in and, without speaking to her, crossed to a safe in the wall below the bookcases, twirled the knob to open it, took out a paper, closed the safe and went out again. So that's where the secrets are, she decided. I can tell Hugh that. As if he didn't know. As if his men haven't already made a minute search of this office and everything in it. She settled back to read the speech.

She was nearly to the end—finding its premises well calculated to irritate liberals and infuriate conservatives—when the hall door was flung open and Jeff Stone strode in.

"Mrs. Mead, here already?" He made no apology for his lateness but shook her hand with a firm grip, moved to the chair behind his desk and pressed a buzzer. "Now I know I'm a man of destiny, since *Background* wants to tell its readers what I think. Yes, I'm back," he told the secretary who came quietly through the door. "I'll take no calls. No interruptions."

"Those letters—" The other man indicated the pile on the desk. "They're an absolute must to go out tonight."

"Fine. I'll sign them in the morning. Any messages that won't keep?"

"Just a call from Senator Mans—"

"That'll keep." A wave of the hand dismissed him and he turned back to Selena. "I liked your husband," he said. "I never could get him to publish my opinions, but sometimes he agreed with them. And when he didn't, we had some good arguments. I was damn sorry when it happened. Okay, you don't want to talk about it. So what is the topic of the day?" He scrabbled among the disarray, found a pink slip. "Oh yes, you're doing an in-depth analysis of Congress. You're only half right. What this place calls for is psychoanalysis."

"You think Congress is sick?"

"Only schizophrenic. Take today. We stayed in session till six o'clock to pass a bill raising federal salaries, including our own. The majority was for it. On a voice vote it would have gone through with a roar. But they forced a roll call, name by name, and more than half the boys chickened out. Not that they don't believe they're overworked and underpaid, but they have serious doubts of their ability to convince their constituents between now and election day. Oh, there's nothing wrong with Congress that a minor operation—like cutting away half the members—wouldn't cure."

"And that, I assume, is not for attribution."

He grinned at her and the craggy face became suddenly boyish. "I read *Background*," he returned. "So I know that's not the kind of quote you quote. Too frivolous. Go ahead, ask some intellectual questions and I'll try for matching answers."

"To start with, do you—"

"Not here," he interrupted. "Since they won't let me raise my pay, I don't intend to put in any more overtime. Besides I can talk more freely over a gin-soaked olive."

"More freely?" she questioned. "Is that possible?" And she felt an odd tremor as he grinned again.

In the dimly lit cocktail lounge he gave his opinions, some of them quotable, of the committee system, the seniority rule, the Rules Committee, the Speaker of the House, the Minority Leader and a dozen other subjects. While he talked she studied him. Jeff Stone was neither tall nor dark nor handsome. Of medium height and slender build, his walk was cocky, his stance almost pugilistic. Untamed sandy hair topped a face whose narrow length ended squarely in a bulldog jaw. Flashes of humor occasionally softened the icy blue of his eyes, gave a half sardonic, half rueful twist to his lips. Even in private his voice rose and fell in subtle nuances that hinted at his power as a spellbinding orator. The blunt-fingered hands that circled the cocktail glass gave an impression of coiled-spring strength. Beebee had spoken of animal magnetism, called him a tiger. Smoldering volcano, Selena thought, might be a more apt phrase.

Abruptly he cut himself short in midsentence, looked at his watch. "Time we had something to eat," he announced. "Can you cook?"

"Yes." She was startled by the abruptness of the question.

"Good. I feel like pushing a basket through a supermarket, dropping in anchovies and odorous cheese while you pick out more plebeian items." He snapped his fingers at the waiter, called for the check while she considered how to answer. It was clearly a program Section Q would endorse. A home-cooked meal and cozy evening *à deux* would be much more conducive to the kind of confidences Hugh wanted than a round of public places. Yet she resented his arrogant assumption that he was in charge, longed to counter with the polite brushoff that, in other circumstances, would be automatic. While her decision hung in balance, he made it easy.

"Funny the things you miss." He was almost wistful. "The sizzles and smells of your own kitchen. Helping yourself from the icebox. Piling dishes in the sink." He dropped a bill and coins on the salver, rose to his feet. "Ready? Let's go."

After dinner they decided the night chill justified a log fire. He lighted it expertly while she poured coffee, set out glasses and cognac. Joining her on the couch, he stared for a minute at the leaping flames, then cocked his head at her.

"It's evenings like this," he said, "that make me realize what a great country we live in."

Her eyes widened at the edge of bitterness that stripped his words of meaning.

"Only in America," he went on, "would a girl like you cook dinner for a guy like me. Take you—your mother's an FFV, your father's a captain of industry, you come from a long line of admirals, landlords and merchant princes. A European education with a Vassar topping."

"You're very well informed."

"I'm very interested, have been for a long time. I used to see you places, sometimes with Simon, sometimes with a group. Until recently, I was lost in the crowd. But you've always stood out from it. And when people talked about you, I listened. So it was easy to collect data, build up the legend.

Big things, like your jilting the broker's son to marry for love. Little things like there being thirty live swans used as decoration for your debut. Medium-sized things like your having gone to school on five continents. Oh, I realized you were out of reach. But I liked knowing you existed. A sort of symbol of all the things I wanted, never had and couldn't get. Now all of a sudden that last part's not so sure. That's what I mean about America."

He paused, gave her a studying glance. She looked back without comment, waited for him to go on.

"We've looked at you," he said; "let's take me. My family's *Mayflower* was a cattle boat and I made my Grand Tour by troopship. I got through college by selling hot dogs at ball games and the GI bill paid the freight at Yale. Yet here I sit"—he lifted the bottle, read from the label—"sipping the brandy of Napoleon as if my ancestors had been landed gentry in the Old South instead of migrants from slum to slum." He looked at her challengingly. "I embarrass you, don't I, with these crude facts. Why? This is democracy in action. We should take pride."

"You don't sound proud."

"Don't I? But I am. I've achieved the American dream. And do you know how? By following the all-American route to the top. I came back from the war with a chestful of medals and a headful of ideals. I studied law in order to help the poor and oppressed, the kind of people I grew up with. Then I went home and opened an office and when business was slow—which was most of the time—I made speeches about the kind of future we should be building. I made so much noise the politicians noticed me and the next thing I was city attorney. I found out the city was full of corruption and began to crack down on gamblers and dope peddlers and grafting cops. The headlines called me a great crusader and one night a group of our most distinguished citizens came to ask me to run for Congress on a reform ticket. Talk about proud!

For me there'll never be another night like that! I won a landslide election and rode off to Washington on my white charger, ready to clean up the country the way I'd cleaned up my home town. Of course, when I got here I learned a fresh-man congressman never gets near the broom closet. And back home the grafters and the grifters moved into position again. I was that naïve! It was a year before I realized that the whole purpose of the reform ticket had been to get me out of town before I uncovered the link between the petty crooks and the power structure and pulled a thread that would un-ravel the whole blanket. That's how democracy works."

"You're very cynical."

"You bet I am. You know what makes a cynic? No, don't give me the Oscar Wilde definition about knowing the price of everything and the value of nothing. That's outdated. To become a cynic today you have to start out as a true believer in the value of big concepts like freedom and brotherhood, honor and integrity, and then find out that there's always somebody ready to buy and sell them at a discount. During my first term I tried to fight the system, but the Establishment has a hundred ways to lasso and hamstring a maverick. Then I worked out my own system. Rock the boat just hard enough to make them nervous but not enough to get tossed over-board. Up to date, it's worked fine. I can't beat them and I won't join them, so I keep my claws and fangs sharp but purr when they pat me. I'm in the market place myself now—and I set a high price."

"How high?"

"Maybe the Senate. Maybe the Vice-Presidency." His laugh was short, humorless. "Maybe something else." He looked at her quizzically. "And along the way I pick up a few dividends. Like this." He put his hand over hers but made no effort to hold on when she pulled it away.

"Is that," she asked crisply, "why you put in such a plea for

42

home cooking? So you could be waited on by an admiral's granddaughter?"

"That was part of my motive. What was yours?"

For an instant she was on guard, wondering if he suspected her real reason for having him here. Then, noting his confident half-smile, she relaxed, said lightly, "You played on my sympathy. I thought you needed to be saved from restaurant meals."

"Lady Bountiful." He bowed in mock deference. "You mean this wasn't democracy at all, but the old feudal system? Pity I've no forelock to pull."

"You don't make fun of democracy in your public speeches, do you?" With difficulty she maintained a casual tone. "Someone might accuse you of communist leanings."

"Oh, it's all right to attack democracy," he retorted, "so long as no derogatory remarks are made against capitalism."

"But you believe in our system," she persisted, "in spite of its flaws? Or would you want to see—"

"How serious we're getting." Again he reached for her hand. A narrowing of his eyes showed awareness of her reaction to the pressure. "Tell me, can you cook breakfast too?"

She left her hand in his, concentrated on trying to slow her pulse. "Is that another of your ambitions?" she asked. "Breakfast with an admiral's granddaughter?"

"I'd like to stay for breakfast with you even if you had no ancestors. But I admit the pedigree is a plus."

"Tomorrow morning," she said firmly, "I intend to eat alone."

"And the next day?" He turned her palm upward, counted off the days on her fingers. "And the next? No doubt you're right. It's my turn to cook for you. I've a little place in the woods that I get away to when the four walls of my room start closing in. How about driving out with me this weekend? I'll barbecue a steak and you won't have to lift a finger till time to wash the dishes."

"Where is it?"

"Far enough to be quiet, peaceful—and completely private."

"Thank you," she said, "but any time you want to cook for me, my kitchen's available. And the dishwasher's automatic."

"Not to mention the little woman who comes in to clean up in the morning. No, I'd like to wait on you in a place that's all my own."

"If you'd tell me the location," she suggested, "it might have more appeal."

"You think you may have friends in the neighborhood? Not a chance. That's the main thing my place has to offer—no neighbors. Now your house—there are probably more office-holders, journalists and cookie pushers with windows on this street than any block in town."

"Whose reputation are you protecting?" she asked. "Yours or mine?"

"You're one of the golden girls," he answered. "Nothing can dim your shine. But I'm strictly silver plate and easy to tarnish. Yes, since you put the question, I'm thinking of myself."

"At least you're truthful."

"At least." His smile grew gentler. "This is true too. You're a very attractive woman. And this must be a lonely time. I've been through a man-breaking year. We could be good for each other. Now will you ride out to the country with me on Saturday?"

"I'm sorry," she said. "I'm not a weekender."

"I'm sure you're not. But every rule has its exception. I thought I might be yours."

"I—I'll think about it. But tomorrow's only Friday. Will I see you then?"

"Tomorrow I fly to the Middle West to make three speeches. I'll phone you from there. Now I think it's time for the windows on your square to see me start for home."

She went with him to the door. He cupped her chin in his

44

hands, looked into her eyes. Then he leaned over to touch his lips lightly to hers.

"Good night, Selena," he said. "Until Saturday."

The phone signal followed so promptly on his exit that it must have been watched and immediately reported to Hugh. But of course, she realized, Jeff was probably under constant surveillance by Section Q. The ringing completed the dash-dash-dot-dash code for Q, but Selena remained unmoving for another minute while she tried to organize her whirling thoughts. What had the evening accomplished? Had she learned anything worth while? It seemed to her that she had floundered, asking none of the right questions, getting no substantial answers. What had she to tell Hugh? And what would his next instructions be? Slowly, with reluctance, she started toward the back garden.

When they were in the den, with Hugh settled back in an easy chair, his long legs stretched out over an ottoman, she was on the defensive. "You should have waited till tomorrow," she told him. "I need time to think, to sort out my impressions."

"I've a busy day tomorrow," he returned. "Anyway, it's your first impressions I want—not a neat, censored, all-loose-ends-tied version."

"I've nothing but loose ends. The only facts I've collected are ones I'm sure you've learned more about from other sources. Like his being heavily in debt and needing money to campaign."

"Yes, we've considerable data on that."

"And you know all about the breakup of his marriage."

"We're building a file on that too," he answered. "Did he tell you his wife's an alcoholic?"

"He didn't talk about her at all. But I heard it from someone else." She detailed her conversation with Beebee, ending with the gossip about Jeff and Gilly.

45

"She knows almost as much as we do," Hugh said wryly. "Which shouldn't surprise me. But I'm glad you got the rumors from a mentionable source. Now you can ask him about them."

"Ask him about Gilly?"

"Sure. It's a natural question. Your friend told you she was his girl, you want to know if it's true. He'll be glad to cast you as a jealous woman checking up on his other affairs. And his reaction may be revelatory. From what you've seen so far, would you say he's a man who'd be putty in the hands of a woman?"

"Never!"

Her vehemence brought a swiftly appraising glance from under his half-closed lids. "You sound pretty positive. What's your basis? Was he immune to your charms?"

"Look here," she flared, "I'm not a *femme fatale*. I don't pretend to be. I don't want to be. This was your idea, not mine, and I'm sure some other woman would be better qualified to—"

"Sorry," he cut in. "I didn't mean to tread on your feelings. But the question still stands and it's important. Why are you so sure Stone is no woman's victim?"

"I'm not sure at all. Maybe he fell madly in love with that— with the Conroy girl. Maybe she had him in such a state that he'd do anything for her. But I don't believe it. It just isn't in character. I don't think anybody—male or female—could push him around. He's determined to be in command, get his own way, give no concessions."

"Hmm. He made quite an impression."

"You asked for my opinion," she said tartly. "So I'm giving it to you, as completely and clearly as I can. He's interested in me and he thinks it's more than reciprocated. What else could he think, since there's no other explanation for all the encouragement I gave him? He was confident he could spend the night here if he wanted to. And he wanted to, I've no doubt of that."

"I don't doubt it either."

"But he picked up his hat and went home while it was still a respectable hour, in case the neighbors were making notes. He's controlled, calculating, never loses sight of his main goal. So it's highly unlikely that he could be cajoled into giving away secrets or walk into a trap that would make blackmail possible."

"So you're downgrading sex as a motive. That leaves money as the strongest contender."

"There's another possibility," she suggested, "that wasn't on your list. He did a lot of talking about his own philosophy."

"He didn't quote Karl Marx?"

"No, it was much more complex. I don't think he's a communist. And I don't believe he's a traitor either. It just doesn't seem possible that he could be."

"The impossible," he quoted, "takes a little longer."

"But if he is, the cause could be—well, something like disappointment. He started out believing the world was made of copybook virtues and got a shock when he found out it's sometimes patched together with deals and compromises. Maybe he decided to hit back, get even with America, with democracy, for destroying his illusions."

"Like a kid on Christmas morning who smashes his toys when he hears there's no Santa Claus? It's an intriguing theory, but I prefer sex and money. The evidence is easier to develop. You're off to a good start. Next time the picture may get clearer. When do you see him again?"

"We don't have a definite date. He's going out of town tomorrow."

"Oh yes. Dinner in Indianapolis, then brunch in Louisville and lunch in Cleveland. But he'll fly back Saturday afternoon."

"I know. He wants me to go with him to his country cabin."

"His cabin?" He swung his feet to the floor and turned to look at her sharply. "That's something we missed. None of the reports showed him owning property in this area. You sure he said he has a cabin?"

"Of course I'm sure."

"What's the location?"

"He was rather evasive when I asked him that. He mentioned its being in the woods. I gathered it's a good distance from Washington and quite isolated."

"If he has a hideaway," Hugh said slowly, "a place nobody knows about, that doesn't show up on any of his records, it could be significant. So find out where it is."

"He won't tell me. The only way I can find out is by going there."

"Then go. You say the invitation is for Saturday night? O.K., I guess I can wait that long for the information. It looks as if my boys are slipping, though, if a man can own a house and land without their knowing anything about it. Have you anything else to report?"

"Only that I don't like this assignment. I don't like it at all. Oh, it's easy enough for you to tell me to go off with him to the country as if all I had to do is check the address and telephone you. It's—it's repugnant to me!"

"I know that. But if the people are going to have fresh water, somebody has to work in the sewers."

"But why me? Can't you find someone who—well, who—"

"Who can do the job and who likes sewers?" he finished for her. "That combination doesn't exist, at least, not on my staff. There's only you, Selena. Now are you leading up to a resignation or just filing a protest?"

"I can't resign," she said unhappily. "Not if it has to be done and there's no one else. Only—"

"You're tired." He got up from the chair, looked down at her sympathetically. "It's been a long, hard day. Get a good night's sleep and give yourself a holiday tomorrow. There's nothing more for you to do till the congressman comes back to town."

She stood up too, put out a hand to stop him as he started to leave. "What about the girl? How is she? The paper I saw at noon ran a sensational biography but nothing new on her condition. Is there any change?"

For answer he pulled from his jacket pocket the late night edition of the morning *Post*, put his thumb on a bulletin in big black type with the headline GILLY CONROY IMPROVES. The brief paragraph stated that the doctor was, for the first time, offering a better than fifty-fifty chance for her recovery. While she was still in a coma, she was gaining strength and there was a strong possibility that she would, within a day or two, recover consciousness.

"Oh I'm glad," Selena said fervently. "I'm very glad."

"We'd be glad too," Hugh seconded, "if it were true." He answered her look of bewilderment. "No, her prospects are no brighter than in the beginning. She's getting weaker. The doctor says it's just a matter of time till her heart stops beating. Maybe a couple of days."

"Then this—" She tapped the paper. "It's all a fabrication?"

"The doctor works for Section Q. We thought a prediction that she's going to recover and will soon be able to talk might smoke out the opposition. They've no reason to think she's being treated differently from any other would-be suicide. So it's possible she'll have some visitors tomorrow. Who knows? Your Mr. Stone may read this and decide to keep the Hoosiers waiting."

CHAPTER THREE

Friday

Give yourself a holiday, Hugh had said, but she was far too restless. She stayed home all morning checking her notes for the *Background* article and after lunch decided to go up to the Capitol for more interviews. Putting out antennae in that atmosphere might pull in some fresh leads on the Joint Committee, Congressman Stone or Gilly Conroy. In the taxi a new plan began taking shape in her mind. It prompted her to make her first stop at the office of the senator from Gilly's state for whom, according to the newspaper biographies, she had worked when she first came to Washington.

A rather plain but effervescent blond girl was typing letters in the outer room. The senator, she said, had gone to the barbershop, should be back within half an hour. Certainly she could wait for him, just sit down and make herself comfortable. Since the girl showed no eagerness to return to her typewriter, Selena commented on the weather, which led to an exchange on climate in general, then to contrasting Washington life with that in a small southern town till it became logical to ask, "Have you been here long?"

"Seven years," the girl—her name, she volunteered, was Marilee—answered. "I finished high school and took a business course and this was my first job."

"Then you must have worked with that poor girl who jumped off the bridge."

"I did, indeed I did." The blue eyes clouded and the accent

thickened till Selena had difficulty understanding all the words. "Back home we were best friends and we came here together. In actual fact, it was after I got this appointment, I said, 'Gilly, why don't you pack up and come along, I don't want to be up North there all alone,' and she allowed she might like Washington, so my daddy talked to the senator and he hired us both. We got a little apartment together and it was real nice. But she only worked here a year and then she started making more money and got a place of her own. You know what I've been thinking the last two days? If I hadn't said that to Gilly, she wouldn't have come here and then maybe—what happened wouldn't have happened. I blame myself, I declare I do."

"You shouldn't," Selena said. "She doesn't sound like the kind of girl who would have stayed home all her life."

"No, she wasn't." Marilee brightened. "Gilly always had big-city ideas. Did you know she was runner-up once to the girl who represented our state in the Miss America contest?"

"Really? I should be pleased to hear that, since some of my friends said they thought the picture in the paper looked like me."

"They did?" Marilee adjusted her spectacles for a better view, gave the matter thoughtful consideration. "You know, I hadn't noticed it, but now I can see there is a resemblance. Of course, Gilly's cheeks were fuller. At least, they used to be, she was inclined to be plump, but she was always careful what she ate. In actual fact, the last time I saw her I thought she was getting downright thin. Yes, I do see a resemblance. Only Gilly was more—you know, sexy?"

"And I suppose you and she talk alike."

"Back home nobody thought so. But after we came here people began mistaking our voices. I think it was because being among all these northern accents made us sound the same. You know, it was funny sometimes. Gilly's boy friends would phone and I'd say she wasn't home and then they'd swear that I was Gilly pretending to be me in order to get out of talking to them."

"And the other way around?"

"Well, not so often. Gilly got most of the calls and I was home more of the time to answer. She was exciting to live with. Always something going on. But she wasn't a bad girl, she really wasn't, not the way the papers make her out. She just wanted—well, to be happy. She liked fun and parties and going to fancy places and pretty clothes and money to spend and—well, men around. But at heart she was good, I do know that. There was a man came to see me last night, a magazine person like you, something called *Candid Confessions*. Did you ever hear of that?"

"It sounds familiar." Probably, Selena added mentally, privately published by Section Q.

"He asked all kinds of questions about her. You know, it's funny. You go along and nobody cares if you're alive and then you do something like—like trying to kill yourself and everybody wants to know what you ate for breakfast. He said his magazine was going to do a big spread on her. I don't know, maybe I shouldn't have told him all I did, but the way I thought is this—reporters have ways of finding out everything anyway, so it's better that he hear about her from a friend."

"Were you able to suggest any reason why she might have wanted to die?"

"Oh no! She wasn't that kind of person at all. Unless—Look, you're not going to write a story about her, are you?"

"My magazine wouldn't be interested. It's a different type from *Candid Confessions*. I'm just personally curious."

"It's natural," Marilee assured her. "When there's a tragedy like this, everybody wants to hear about it. My goodness, the last two days, I've had calls from people I was totally out of touch with, just because they knew I knew Gilly."

"You started to say," Selena prompted, "something about her reason."

"I didn't say this to the *Confessions* writer—well, I wouldn't say it to any man, even if he wasn't a reporter. But I do believe Gilly was going to have a baby."

"Oh." Selena felt herself go cold. "Did she tell you that?"

"No, I haven't talked to Gilly for ages. We don't see much of each other nowadays. She's always so busy and—well, our lives are different. So I'm just guessing. But I know the kind of person she was. She loved being alive, she really did. No matter how wrong things went, she was never down for more than a minute. Oh, she'd complain, make a lot of thunder, but then she'd say, "Tomorrow it'll all come up roses," and be cheerful again. So I know, I absolutely know that no ordinary trouble could make her do it. It had to be—that kind of trouble."

"Have you any pictures of her?"

"I did have, lots of snapshots. But I gave them all to the *Candid Confessions* man. He talked me into letting him have her scrapbook too, the one she started in high school. Gilly left it behind when she moved out of the apartment, told me to throw it out, but I didn't. You know something else of hers I have? A phonograph record. I remembered it after the man left last night. I guess it was getting him the scrapbook that put it into my mind. And I took it out and played it. Gilly made it when she was practicing for the talent part of the beauty contest. She gave a scene from the play *Macbeth*. By William Shakespeare. It seemed so strange to be listening to her voice again. But I'm mighty glad to have it now. And I hope the man sends back the book and pictures, the way he promised. I wouldn't want to lose them, especially if she—" She shook off the word before she said it, went on positively, "Gilly isn't going to die, though. Today, for the first time, there was good news."

"Yes, the morning paper was quite optimistic."

55

"And I called the hospital, too, to ask about her. I thought if she's so much better, I might be able to go and see her."

"What did you find out?"

"They connected me right away with her private nurse. And she was very encouraging. She said Gilly wasn't ready for company yet, she's still unconscious. But they think very soon, maybe even tomorrow, she'll be able to talk again. The nurse asked me my name and how I knew Gilly so when she wakes up she can tell her I was inquiring. And she even wrote down my number, because she said before long Gilly might be able to use the phone herself. Now that's a good sign, isn't it?"

"It seems to be." She changed the subject. "Does she have any family back home?"

"Her parents are dead. She has one brother, but he was a lot older and they were never close. He went off and joined the navy when Gilly was about twelve. Mostly, she lived with an aunt."

She went on then to talk, under Selena's apparently aimless questioning, of growing up together and of the months in Washington before their paths separated. The recital continued till the senator, pink and glowing from his massage, returned to greet Selena warmly and conduct her into his office.

"Did I have an appointment with you?" he asked. "It's not on my book and I'm sure if I'd made it, I could never forget it."

"No, I just dropped by on the chance of finding you in."

"I'm almost always in," he said, "except when it's my turn to put my finger in the dike to hold back the flood of their so-called Civil Rights bill. They kept us here till seven o'clock last night and now they say they're going to hold sessions on Saturdays too. We're old men and they think they can wear us out. Well, we've taught them before and we'll teach them again. But you're wrongheaded on this too, aren't you, Selena?" He shook his head sadly. "A collateral descendant of

General Robert E. Lee gone over to the Yankees! Well, we won't go into such unpleasantness."

"It's what I'm here for," she answered. "I need your views on the filibuster for my magazine."

He gave them to her eloquently and at length. She listened without interruption. When he ran down she closed her notebook and thanked him.

"Incidentally," she added, "your receptionist is a very nice girl. She kept me from being bored while I waited."

"I guarantee I can tell you her subject. She has only one these days. Being acquainted with Gilly Conroy has put considerable spice in Marilee's life."

"You knew her too, didn't you?"

"She sat out there"—he waved toward the outer room— "and in a few months managed to throw my entire filing system into utter confusion. I admit she added a degree of pulchritude to the office, but her mind wasn't on the work. And now do you know what the papers back home are saying? 'Senator's Ex-Secretary Attempts Suicide.' It's six years since she was in my employ, but I'm responsible. It doesn't sound good, especially in an election year. However, I guess I shouldn't hold it against poor Gilly. She wasn't meaning to do me harm. In actual fact, she was a girl who wouldn't harm anybody on purpose. Although I did hear something about her recently that shocked me very much."

"What was that?"

"I was told that she sometimes worked for the Republicans."

"Not really!"

"Oh, not often, I feel sure. She did most of her spying for us."

"Spying?"

"You understand how it is, Selena. Bits and pieces of information can be mighty useful on the legislative front. What goes on in a caucus. Whose vote is wavering. When an amendment is going to be introduced. Oh, a girl like Gilly who has a wide assortment of friends and knows how to listen can earn a good day's pay. In actual fact, we could use her help right now to wangle out some of the other side's strategy."

"On the other hand," Selena said mischievously, "she might help them to wangle out yours."

"That's the danger," he conceded. "She could even be working for both at once. To tell you the truth, I don't think that girl had any political convictions. To her it was all just a job. If a man paid her to find out something, she didn't care if he was a Democrat, a Republican or a lobbyist. To do her credit, I don't think she was ever intentionally disloyal. She just never realized that she was betraying her own people."

"That's a charitable way of looking at it."

"But you didn't come here to hear me ramble on about Gilly Conroy. Is there anything else you need for your article?"

"No, you've covered the subject very thoroughly."

"Don't misquote me now," he warned. "What I said was: The people who talk the most about freedom are attacking the basic cornerstone of freedom in the free world. Freedom of speech in the United States Senate. What do you think of that?"

"I think," she rose to leave, "that you'll sweep your state in the next election."

"You're a saucy girl." He patted her cheek. "Give my greetings to your dear mother."

When she was once more in her own home she phoned the secret number through which it was always possible, day or night, to get word to Hugh. Sometimes he answered himself. More often someone else was there with instructions on how and where he could be reached. If he was not near a phone, his assistant could, by pushing a button, activate a mechanism in his watch to summon him to contact the office. That watch—in appearance, the old-fashioned pocket model—was one more source of hilarity to his friends. Sometimes at a party the soft buzzer would sound. "My alarm," he'd say, take out the watch and look at it. "Yes, it's time to go home," or, if it suited the occasion better, "Time to make a phone call," or even "Time to take a pill." And as he ambled away, laughter would explode behind him at "poor old Hugh" and his eccentricities. The arrangement worked with such precision that Selena was used to getting in touch with him in minutes, never more than an hour. But this time, after she identified herself, the girl asked, "Is it an emergency? Do you need help at once?"

"Oh no. I just have a few things to tell him. And there's something I'd like him to get for me. But there's no hurry about any of it."

"That's good. Because he's likely to be occupied till very late, perhaps all night. So if you can wait till tomorrow—"

"I can, easily. Just tell him that, if he has some time in the morning, I'd like to see him."

CHAPTER FOUR

Saturday

Her breakfast table was in an alcove of the kitchen made by a bay window that overlooked her front door. She sipped coffee and read the morning paper. Gilly, it said, was continuing to improve, showing flickers of returning consciousness. Such medical details as the steadying of her heartbeat, the refraction of her pupils gave the story substance. Even Selena's contrary knowledge faltered in the face of the solid black type, the physician's confident quotes. She must be getting better, she thought. Soon she'll be able to talk, to solve the case without further help from me. It's been hours since this paper went to press. Perhaps even now she's conscious again, beginning to tell Section Q exactly what happened.

From a street outside her window Hugh's voice cut across her thoughts.

"Going down to the canal," he was shouting to the man next door. "Want to do a sketch of Key Bridge from a point near Bailey's Boathouse."

"Your name is legion," the neighbor retorted. "Every artist in town has done that view."

"But never with the special Hugh Pierce touch."

"How true! Yours won't resemble anyone else's. In fact, it won't even resemble a bridge."

Selena looked out to see him trudge on without a glance toward her window. He assumed she'd be listening, ready to follow. Twenty minutes later, in the role of a morning exerciser, she strolled along the canal to the point he had indicated, found him comfortably settled against a bank making rapid brush strokes on a sketch pad. She sat down behind him, looking critically from pad to bridge, but made no comment.

"You've a few things to tell me, something you want me to get." He repeated her message, waited for her to carry on.

"None of it urgent," she supplemented. "So I hope you'll tell me what you were doing last night. Had it something to do with this case?"

"These days everything in Section Q has to do with this case. It's top priority."

"Were you with Gilly? Did she talk?"

"Yes, I was with her—at least, I was at the hospital. No, she didn't talk. And she isn't about to. I thought I explained that."

"You did, but that was night before last. I hoped maybe by now—after all, doctors can make mistakes."

"And there are such things as miracles," he countered. "In Gilly's case, that's what it will take. So if you're praying, don't stop. Her recovery would certainly simplify our problem. But it's our slimmest hope."

"Then last night—"

"Last night we used her to bait a trap. Or rather we used the news that she'd soon start talking. We hoped a rat might walk in."

"Did it work?"

"We caught a mouse. A non-squealing one, unfortunately. From the beginning we've had Gilly under tight security. The nurses, the orderlies, everybody who enters her room is part of Section Q. We figured the opposition would have cased the pattern, so the night nurse had a regular 1 A.M. coffee break when they could count on Gilly's being left alone for a quarter of an hour."

"But wouldn't they expect her to be guarded?"

"You forget. This is just a girl who got tired of living and jumped off a bridge. That's all they know we know. No reason to give her special protection. Anyway, with the papers forecasting recovery, they had to chance it. And they minimized the risk to themselves to almost zero. Last night two minutes after the nurse walked out a man in white walked in. The only way to tell him from an intern was the silent gun in his pocket."

"He got into Gilly's room?"

"She's in a suite. You pass through an empty room on the way to hers. He got only as far as the first room—which wasn't quite empty. My boys had him in hand and out of there before the nurse sugared her coffee."

"Then you've captured one of them."

"We've captured a hired gun," Hugh corrected. "Who knows nothing. At least, that's the story he stuck with through a long hard night. I think it's the truth."

"But at least he knows who hired him."

"Sure he does. A man named John Smith who phoned him and set up a rendezvous on a park bench after dark. He gave him step-by-step instructions and a thousand dollars in cash."

"But would they turn anything so important over to a complete stranger?"

"The gunman was no stranger. I'm sure they investigated him thoroughly. We know his record too—he's a very proficient worker. Last night was one of his few failures."

"And they paid him in advance? How could they know he wouldn't take their money and do nothing for it?"

"In that kind of deal, there has to be trust on one side. And a man isn't likely to take a job like that from an anonymous boss on credit. Anyway, he's a killer, not a thief. And if he reneged, his name would go on another G-note passed to another gunman. It's a system designed to keep a man honest— and fixes it so that if one is caught he has no information. Of course we're holding on to him, using all our means of persuasion. He may produce a few more details about John

Smith, but the odds are against his knowing much more than he's already told us."

"The morning paper still talks about her regaining consciousness. Do you think they'll try again?"

"It's a possibility. They have no way of knowing what happened last night. It could be their man tried to beat the system and skipped with the money. So they might try again with one of their own people, which could be a big lift up for us. But they're probably too cagey for that. One thing last night established beyond doubt, though, is that Gilly has knowledge that's dangerous to them. Her imminent recovery is making them nervous. And nervous men make mistakes. So we'll keep scratching them with that needle. But most of our eggs are in other baskets. Like yours. What have you heard from Congressman Stone?"

"Nothing yet. That isn't why I called you. I went up to the Hill yesterday and talked with a couple of people who knew Gilly."

"She's not your assignment." He held his brush at arm's length and sighted along it. "I have her past, present and future—if any—well covered."

"I'm sure you have. But one of the men on my list to interview for the magazine is the senator who brought her to Washington. So I thought I might pick up a little extra information."

"And did you?"

In condensed form she passed along Marilee's statement, concluding, "But I expect you know all that."

"Yes, I do."

"One thing she didn't tell your man, though, is that she thinks the reason Gilly tried to kill herself is because she was pregnant."

"Since it's false, it's not very useful."

"Are you sure she wasn't?"

"Of course I'm sure. But we're not looking for a motive for

suicide, so it doesn't really matter." He gave her a sharp glance. "Unless it matters to you."

"You told me not to sift the evidence," she said hastily, "but to pass on everything, whether or not I thought it was important. I didn't really expect to learn anything from Marilee. I was mainly interested in hearing her talk, studying her accent. But the senator said something that might be significant. He was talking about her work for different factions on the Hill, even including Republicans. He said he didn't think she had any political beliefs, that she could work for both sides without any notion of being disloyal."

"Are you suggesting that she might spy for the Reds on the same basis? No, Selena, nobody's that confused. The senator might not recognize it, but there's a big gap between disloyalty to the Confederacy and national treason. If Gilly was getting information for the communists, it wasn't because she thought they were just one more political party."

"No," she said slowly. "No, I suppose not. Only if she—if she's going to die—"

"*De mortuis nil nisi bonum?* Well, she's not dead yet. And we don't plan to write 'traitor' on her tombstone. But we have to deal with facts, whatever they are, whomever they hurt. What others have you?"

"None," she answered. "Only a request. Do you think you could get me the record Marilee mentioned? The one of Gilly as Lady Macbeth."

"If she played it last night, it's probably still on her turntable. It would be easy to pick up. Why do you want it?"

"It's just an idea. Probably nothing will come of it. I'll tell you about it later."

"What do you mean by later? After you've acted on your own, set wheels in motion that it's too late to slow down?"

"Of course not. I just don't want to talk about it now because it might sound stupid. There's no point in going into it until it appears that it could be practical and worth while.

But naturally I'll clear it with you first. I'd have to. What I have in mind can't be done without your full approval and cooperation. So don't worry about that."

"All right." He put down his brush and turned round to study her speculatively. "I'll get the record for you. But I want this clearly understood. You're working under orders—not inspiration. Talking to the senator and the girl yesterday did no harm, but it's duplication and we haven't time for that. You've one specific job. Jeffrey Stone."

"I understand your orders perfectly," she retorted. "I'm to go to the country with him tonight."

"I didn't issue that order," he said. "I asked you to find out where his cabin is. If you can get that information without leaving town, it'll suit me fine. Just remember, Selena, this game is for life-and-death stakes. And if any player goes off-side, it can foul the whole team."

"I won't forget." She stood up, brushed dirt and twigs from her skirt. "Now I'll go home and wait for a call from Cleveland."

She resumed work on her article, had it nearly finished when, in late afternoon, the call came. Stone was, he said, at the Cleveland airport.

"Take-off in ten minutes." His speech was clipped. "Land at National at five thirty-one. My secretary will pick you up at five sharp, drive you out to meet me. Got that?"

"At five sharp." She was caught up in his tempo, could do no more than repeat his words. "Yes, I have it."

"Fine, see you then. Got to run."

He rang off, leaving her half stunned, still holding the receiver. Everybody, she thought wryly, is giving me orders. He must think he has me hypnotized. I wish I could tell him I'm meeting his plane for only one reason. Because he's suspected of being a spy. But it wasn't suspicion that quickened her pulse as she began to dress or dictated the choice of the fuzzy wool of palest lavender that brought out answering tones in her eyes and sharpened the contrast between ivory skin and raven hair. She was ready a few minutes early, used the time to dial the Section Q number. This time a man answered, but not Hugh.

"Just tell him," she left the message, "that I'm meeting the five thirty-one from Cleveland at National Airport."

The secretary was punctual. He was driving the bright red sports model in which she'd ridden with the congressman two nights earlier. He was a thin-lipped intense-looking young man who answered her attempts at conversation politely but without enthusiasm. Is this, she wondered, one of his frequent functions—taking women to meet the master? And did he know about the country cabin? She shriveled a little at the thought, recoiled from introducing the subject. Yet it was probable that he did know and could tell her its location. Once she had that information, the whole evening's program could be altered. So she made herself say casually, "Congressman Stone said something about having a place in the country. Is it in Virginia?"

This time he did take his eyes from the wheel long enough to give her a look of full comprehension. "I think the congressman plans to show it to you tonight," he said with a finality that cut off further questions.

She felt the blood rise hotly to her cheeks, shrank back against the cushions. I've a job to do, she told herself fiercely, an important job. What earthly difference does it make what this man thinks of me? Anyway, I'm not committed to the cabin yet. The secretary will have to be driven back to Washington and before we start out again I'll insist on learning where he's taking me. There's nothing illogical about refusing to leave for an unknown destination. It was probably only a whim that kept him from telling me before. There's no reason for him to conceal the address—unless he really has something to hide, something serious.

From Hugh's report of the hired gunman she had salvaged one fact. The park bench meeting had taken place after dark. He hadn't specified the day, but it seemed probable that it had immediately preceded the attack on Gilly. If that was so and if Jeff had kept his dinner date in Indianapolis, one thing was proved. He could not be John Smith. The conclusion gave her a strange lift of spirits so that she was able to glance at the immobile profile beside her and wonder with near detachment what was in his mind.

They arrived at the airport well in advance of the plane's arrival. She sat near a window while the secretary paced the area between the ticket counters. When the landing was announced they moved separately to the specified gate. He continued his pacing while she stood by the glass to watch the great silver ship taxi to a stop. Jeff was the first to debark. He bounded down the steps, started across the field, his eyes searching the waiting crowd. Then, as he sighted her, his whole face lighted in—the comparison surprised her—childlike delight. He broke into a near run and she found herself involuntarily moving toward him. He put out his left hand to seize her right in an almost bone-crushing grip, then loosened but did not release it as they started back to the lobby.

"I didn't think you'd come," he said.

"You didn't?" she faced him, unbelieving. "I thought you took it for granted. You didn't give me a chance to refuse."

"Strategy!" He laughed happily. "Never offer an alternative."

"Does it always work?" she asked. "With both women and politics?"

"You're here," he returned. "That's the answer for today."

As they climbed the stairs the secretary came up unobtrusively on his other side, spoke in a voice too low for Selena to hear. Jeff answered with a curt, "Right" and exchanged

69

baggage check for key chain. At the top the other man turned aside to the baggage room while Jeff conducted Selena through the lobby and out to the parking lot. He helped her in, went round and slid behind the wheel. It was not till he started the motor that she realized his intention.

"What about him?" she demanded. "Your secretary. You're not leaving him behind?"

"Three's a crowd." He shifted into reverse.

"How will he get home?"

"There are taxis, buses, limousines." He grinned at her concern. "If he's feeling adventurous, he can hitchhike."

"But isn't he getting your suitcase? Don't you need it?"

"I don't plan to wear a dinner jacket tonight. Travers will take the bag to my hotel and leave it. How he gets there is his problem. Why are you so worried about him? He's a very unappealing type."

"It's just that—well, it doesn't seem very considerate to drive off and leave him like this."

"I'm an inconsiderate employer. All my staff will testify to that. Besides, Washington is thataway." He jerked a thumb to the right. "We're headed in the opposite direction."

"You're not driving back to Washington?"

"Is that where you want to go?" He had backed into the traffic lane. Now he pulled to one side, let the motor idle.

"I—I hadn't thought—" She studied her hands in her lap, at a loss for an answer. "You were on and off the phone so fast."

"Yes, that was a short conversation. But we had a long talk the other night. I thought you might not come today. But I assumed that if you did it would mean you were willing to visit my little hut."

"Where is it? Can you show it to me on the map?"

"Why this emphasis on geography? I can show it to you on the ground. We'll be there in twenty minutes."

"First I'd like to know where we're going. Is that so unreasonable?"

"Yes, I think it's your way of stalling. This isn't a kidnaping, Selena. If you say you want to go home, I'll take you there. If you don't—well, the decision is yours to make."

He sat watching her while she hesitated. The decision, she thought, isn't mine. It's Section Q's. So there's only one answer.

"All right," she said, then added inanely, "since it's so close."

"Right." Perhaps tactfully, he said no more, didn't look at her but concentrated on maneuvering out of the parking lot and onto the road. He had pushed the button that swung back the car's top and as they reached the highway she became aware of a helicopter hovering above them. She was instinctively sure that it contained Q-men. So Hugh had her under observation, would be told where she was as soon as the car stopped. Her second thought was less flattering. It was, of course, the congressman who was being followed. Her whereabouts was of far less interest to Q than that of his cabin. Jeff did not appear to notice the copter. Nor, unless he was already apprehensive, was there reason for him to, since flying objects were commonplace in that sky. When, after about a mile, they turned off the main highway, it continued to go straight ahead, but she was sure it still had the red car in view.

"You took a dinner jacket to Indianapolis?" she said to break the silence. "Was it a black-tie banquet?"

"It was a hundred dollars a plate," he answered. "That's worth dressing up for. How did you know I was in Indianapolis last night?"

"Why—you told me you were going there."

"No, I said I was going to the Middle West. And today I phoned you from Cleveland. I never mentioned Indianapolis."

"Didn't you?" She kept her tone disinterested, remembering too late that it was from Hugh she'd heard of the Indiana city. "Then I must have read something in the newspaper about your making a speech there. You did speak, didn't you?"

"Rabblerousingly. Where did you read about it?"

"I don't remember, but it must have been the *Post* or the *Star*. Those are the only papers I've seen today."

"Then my office will have the clipping."

"It may have been a news broadcast," she said desperately. "I have a vague recollection of hearing you were in Indianapolis, but I don't know how. I still think you told me yourself. But what difference does it make? You really were there and it was no secret."

"I hope it was no secret," he amended. "That's why I'm interested in your source. With so many contenders for the top job, it's hard for us second-stringers to squeeze out a paragraph among the want ads. If my talk was reported by the wire services or on a network broadcast, that could be a breakthrough. It's like the first crocus in the spring. I keep looking for signs that there's something growing."

"Then I'm sorry not to be more accurate. The more I think about it, though, the more it seems to me it was on the 11 o'clock news. But I have no idea what station I was tuned to."

"What hurts," he said reproachfully, "is that you could hear the sound of my name and not be instantly alert to every detail."

"It had the opposite effect." She was glad to match his switch to flippancy. "I was so bedazzled, it drove everything else out of my mind."

He laughed, swung the wheel sharply to the left. Their route had, with each turn, become progressively less "main." Now they were on a narrow road, hardly more than a trail, thickly lined with trees. His reference to a place in the woods had, it seemed, been strictly literal. The helicopter was no longer visible and Selena began to worry that she had mistaken its affiliation and purpose. They had made so many twists and turns, left the landmarks so far behind that she would have great difficulty pinpointing the place on a map, could certainly never find it again alone. Unless the bird-men were watching and reporting the car's direction, her trip might prove entirely fruitless.

One more turn brought them to a clearing. In the center was a two-story white house, in appearance no more than a few years old.

"It really is a hideaway," she commented. "There can't be anybody for miles around."

"That's what makes it so ideal." He didn't say for what. She didn't ask him.

Only the location was unconventional. On the inside the house was a duplicate of hundreds in the city. He took her coat, paid tribute with lifted eyebrows to her costume.

"Sit down, put your feet up," he said. "This is my night to work."

Yet there was, as it turned out, little to do. In the living room a fire was laid so the touch of a match started it going. In the dining room two places were set. And, trailing him to the kitchen, she found advance preparations at a stage where broiling the steak, adding dressing to a salad and heating a casserole would complete the meal.

"Catered by leprechauns?" she suggested.

"No, by my secretary. The one we made walk home." He crushed ice, spilled it into a shaker, poured rum over it. "I phoned him from Louisville, gave him instructions."

"I thought you were in Cleveland."

"That was this afternoon. I had my morning coffee in Louisville. At ten dollars a cup."

"You had him bring all this out here before you called me? Even though you doubted that I'd come."

"Doubt everything—but act as if you believed. That's my success secret." He added lime juice and sugar to the ice and rum, began shaking. "I had nothing to lose but a head of lettuce. And I didn't lose. Bring the glasses, will you? Oh yes, my orders also included canapés. They should be on ice."

She looked into the refrigerator, found a foil-covered platter and added it to the tray on which napkins and glasses were already arranged.

"Mr. Travers is very versatile." She took the foil from the collection of varishaped tidbits.

"He has a versatile delicatessen." Still pumping the shaker vigorously, he led the way to the front of the house.

"Cabin is a modest word for this." Seated on the couch, she looked round the large room where pine paneling was the only bow to the rustic setting. "Have you had it long?"

"Long enough." He finished pouring, put a glass in her hand, picked up his own. He looked at her, seemed to be considering a choice of toasts, decided on none. He leaned over to touch the rim of her glass with his, took a contemplative sip. The duration of the pause indicated that he intended no more precise answer to her question, so she let it drop. While they drank he gave highlights of his Midwestern swing.

"I made a hairsbreadth entrance at the banquet last night," he reported. "I was almost out the door when one of my constituents got me on the phone. The fund-contributing kind it's not smart to cut off before he runs down. He talked just long enough to make me miss my plane. So I had to thumb an Air Force jet. Luckily they happened to have one about to take off in the right direction."

"That's a familiar kind of luck—when you happen to be on the committee that handles their appropriation."

"Now who's a cynic? Anyway, I got to Indianapolis, had a motorcycle escort from the airfield to the banquet hall and raced up to the platform as the master of ceremonies was starting to explain my inexplicable absence."

"Was dinner over? Didn't you get anything to eat?"

"Not a bite. That's why I'm ravenous tonight."

He began a semiserious discourse on the psychological benefits of a photo-finish arrival while she did mental arithmetic. Was Indianapolis in a different time zone from Washington? Was 10 P.M. here 9 P.M. there? What time would the eating end and the speaking begin? Could he— this was the crucial question—have been in a Washington park "after dark"? None of the questions had answers. She could only try to banish them by assuring herself that he had volunteered the story of his late departure. The very fact that he had, without necessity, told her about it should in itself be proof that it was no indication of guilt. Unless her slip in mentioning Indianapolis had put him on guard, led him into elaborate explanation of a delay he thought she already knew about. The possibility restrained her from a direct query about the time the Air Force plane took off.

"Hey!" he complained. "Your mind's wandering. I expect a small smile of appreciation for my announcement that if nominated, I will run and if elected, I will not serve. That's a witticism."

"Sorry." She pulled herself back to full attention. "I thought you were simply describing the historical role of all Vice-Presidents."

"That's the trouble with you journalists," he accused. "You're bored with everything but sensational revelations."

"Then make some," she challenged.

"Maybe I will. Maybe I'll tell you my deepest, darkest secret, one I've never confessed to a living soul. Ah, that gets the faraway look out of your eyes. I thought it would."

"Naturally. All women love secrets." He was joking, she knew. But still— "Do tell me."

"Later perhaps, if I'm sure I can trust you. I'd be putting

75

myself entirely in your power, you know. Let my opponents get wind of this and politically, I'm dead."

"You make me very curious."

"I intended to," he said. "I like to be listened to when I talk. But now I'll leave you alone with your curiosity while I turn into a master chef."

"Mind if I explore? I'm also curious about houses."

"There's nothing to see," he discouraged. "It's a very ordinary place."

"I'll just wander about," she persisted and he made no further objection.

It was, as he said, ordinary, though not for one man's country cabin. Both living room and dining room were oversize. The kitchen equipment was adequate for a small embassy. Upstairs she found four rooms, three of them simply but attractively furnished as bedrooms. The door to the fourth was locked. From the bag hanging over her arm she took out her cosmetics kit, found in it the nail file and scissors set that was specially made for picking locks. In less than a minute the door was open and, feeling a little like Bluebeard's wife, she reached out to push it wide. There can't be anything important here, she told herself. If it were anything really damaging, there'd be a more complicated lock.

She put away the manicure set, took out her lipstick. Pressing a tiny button at the side of the metal case produced a beam of light that picked up dust particles in the farthest corner of the room, its power belying the case's small size. She found a light switch, flicked it on, returned the lipstick-flashlight to the kit and the kit to her purse and surveyed the room in which she stood. It was a laboratory—no, a darkroom, she decided, equipped for photographic development. So Jeff's an amateur photographer; there's nothing hidden here, it's locked only to protect the equipment.

Going farther in she found that, except for the equipment and supplies, the room was totally empty. No pictures,

76

no negatives, no film. The bareness made her look more closely and her eye was caught by a jagged triangle of dark blue paper that protruded from a boxlike machine in one corner. It was, she found on closer inspection, a copying machine that operated on something like a roller-towel principle. The paper to be reproduced was placed face down on the transparent surface. The finished copy then came out through a slit in the front where a knife-edge projection made possible a clean cutoff. But the last person using it had, in haste or carelessness, made a not quite clean cut and left behind a small remnant of his copy.

Using the sharp edge with great care, Selena pulled it free, looked down at a crisscrossing of white lines on the blue background. So intent was her examination that she missed the sound of footsteps, jumped when Jeff's voice boomed out behind her.

"So here you are," he said as she turned to face him. "I thought they kept this room—" He stopped, reworded the sentence. "Wasn't the door locked?"

"I can't walk through locked doors," she answered lightly. She closed her fingers over the piece of paper. If he had seen it, he gave no sign, said only, "Let's not keep the steaks waiting. You can see the rest of the house later." He bowed with mock formality, offered her his arm and they walked together down the stairs.

At dinner the talk was first about the article she was writing, then of her work generally, finally became more personal.

"You took on your husband's job without a break, didn't you? Started right to work. That was smart. Having commitments and deadlines must have helped you over the rough spots."

"Yes," she agreed. "It helped considerably."

"You're all alone? No children?" It was more statement than question.

"In the present circumstances," she said, "I guess I should regard that as fortunate."

"Very. When things go wrong, we can take it. We're tough. It's the kids that get hurt. They're so damned vulnerable."

She followed his train of thought. "You have a daughter, haven't you? Is she with her mother?"

"No!" His jaw set in hard lines. "And she's never going to be. Never!" He took a breath, forced a rueful half smile. "Sorry, I didn't mean to explode at you, but you struck a nerve. Deborah's fourteen. I had her in a boarding school, but she ran away twice. The second time there was a boy involved and the school wouldn't let her come back. I've got to do something about her, do it fast. But there's so much happening, so many balls to keep in the air."

"Where is she now?"

"With my sister on the Coast. But that's no solution, not even a temporary one. Oh, Sis tries hard, she does her best. But she has her hands full with four of her own, and Deb's a hard-rock problem. God! how could she be anything else, considering how she grew up. Day after day coming home from school to find the dishes in the sink, dust an inch thick and her mother locked in her room with a sick headache. Deb was on her own from the time she was six. She thinks bananas and cookies are a normal meal."

He stopped, stared fixedly at the flickering candles. Selena felt an urge to reach out and put a hand over his, to say something in comfort. But no words came and it was he who, after a silence, spoke again.

"I'm not shifting the blame." His eyes stayed on the candles. "A lot of it, maybe most of it, was mine. I wasn't there when I should have been. And when I did go home, I was too wound up in what was wrong between my wife and me to give a thought to what we were doing to the kid. My concern came pretty late. But I'm concerned now, deeply and completely. Something good's got to happen to her. Only—" Determination ebbed from his voice, gave place to perplexity. "I don't know what to do. She can't stay with my sister; that's only a stopgap."

"Doesn't her mother want her?"

"You bet she does. At least she's hell-bent on getting her away from me. But that's out, definitely out. Deb's never going to lead her mother's kind of life again. But getting her away from that isn't enough. I've got to put something bright in its place."

"Can't you bring her back to live with you?"

"In a hotel room? Or in a house with a hired housekeeper? Or shunt her off to another boarding school in winter and a camp in the summer? Those are the choices, the way things are now." He raised his eyes to look at her directly. "You accused me the other night of having an ulterior motive for cultivating you. Maybe my subconscious was even more ulterior. You'd be great for Deb."

She flinched from the intensity of his gaze, tried to inject a note of lightness.

"Because I'm an admiral's granddaughter?"

"No, because you're you." He noticed her withdrawal, smiled suddenly. "How's that for a proposal? Will you be my daughter's stepmother?"

"At least, it's novel. But not very romantic."

"And not appropriate to the occasion either. I didn't bring you here tonight to discuss my family troubles. But it's your own fault—you're much too good a listener. And they're never entirely out of my mind. They can't be. I have to make a plan." Again his face darkened. "One thing's for sure, I'm going to win this fight with my wife, get Deb away from her permanently. The kid's never had a chance and she's entitled to one. I'll do anything, anything at all, to see that she gets it."

"Anything?" The word jerked Selena back to her own reason for being there, her need to discover to what lengths Jeff would go, might have already gone, but he misinterpreted the sharpness of her question.

"Not only unromantic," he said, "but ungallant." Mercurially, his spirits rose. "To follow so clumsy a proposal with the suggestion that it sprang from a spirit of self-sacrifice. If I weren't sure your life has been a steady diet of compliments and gallantry, I'd be more contrite. But I want to be remembered as the one who was different."

"You will be," she assured him. "There's no doubt about that."

"Then let's have a change of venue," he said. "And a change of subject. Come into my parlor and I'll find some other ways to prove that I'm unlike the common run of men."

Sitting close to her on the couch, he poured crème de menthe into iridescent glasses. This time he had a cryptic toast, "To the next chapter." His eyes, low-lidded, held hers for an extended minute to give it meaning.

He took a slow sip of the liqueur, put down his glass. He reached for her hand, spread the fingers and examined it closely in a parody of palm reading.

"Firelight becomes you," he said. "You're light and shadow too. So much that's known about you, all the glare of publicity. And behind it an area that's unknown, still to be explored."

His left hand cradled hers and, with his right forefinger, he traced the lines in her palm. His touch was light, faintly tickling. She strove for rigid control, resolved to give him no sign of the tremors it evoked. It was essential that she keep the conversation going, fend off as long as possible the suggestion of another change of place, this time to an upper room. Her duty was to make the evening productive of information. And then— Then what? At that moment she wavered in her answer. That abyss must be crossed later and would, she realized now, be deepened by her own uncertain feelings. She let her hand stay in his but, under cover of setting down her glass, shifted position so that, though seeming to turn toward him, she was actually in less close proximity, their shoulders no longer touching. If he noticed her stratagem, he showed it only in a quick tilting of his eyebrow.

"Light and shadow make a proper setting for secrets," she suggested. "Are you ready to tell me yours?"

"Still gnawing on that?" he teased. "I think I'll draw out the suspense a while longer."

"If you do," she returned, "I won't be able to think of another thing all evening."

"Ah, I can't have that! It seems I've painted myself into a corner where I'll have to tell you. But you realize it will ruin me if you ever let it out."

"Wild horses, et cetera," she declared.

"Then here it is." His voice sank to a sepulchral whisper. "My middle name"—he paused dramatically—"is Rolland."

"Your middle name—" She stared at him uncomprehendingly.

"My mother was a romantic, a reader of English novels. She thought Jeffrey Rolland had a lovely sound. But you can imagine the puns, the slogans, if they were to find out about the Rolland. I couldn't even run for dogcatcher."

"Rollin' Stone, of course." Understanding dawned. "Yes, it would be a handicap."

"You're let down." He looked at her sagely. "You were really expecting an exposé. What did you think I was going to say—that I peddle dope outside high schools?"

"No, I—" Reluctantly, she took advantage of the opening. "I thought you might be going to tell me about your connection with the girl who was found under Calvert Bridge the other night—Gilly Conroy."

"What do you know about her?"

"Beebee Coles—you know, the columnist—told me she was a friend of yours."

"I know her."

"Beebee gave me the impression you spent a lot of time together."

"Tell her," he returned grimly, "that I'm grateful to her for spreading the news by word of mouth instead of in her column. It's not the kind of publicity I'm aiming for."

"That's what makes a place like this so useful, isn't it? Your comings and goings can't be seen and reported."

"Go on. What are you driving at?"

"Just something that occurred to me. You asked me here on such short notice and yet had everything arranged just so. I can't help wondering if you hadn't planned it earlier and then called me in as substitute—after Gilly was hurt."

"My God!" he exploded. "Women! Aren't any of you happy unless you're making yourself miserable?"

"You sound as if the answer to my question is yes."

"It ought to be," he snapped. "It's the only answer that kind of question deserves. But it happens to be false. Sure, it was short notice. I took a chance on being able to get this— to make all the arrangements. And it worked out fine. I run an efficient shop."

"And the routine, I expect, is well established."

"All right," he said resignedly, "since you're determined to scrape the file across the board. Yes, Gilly's been here with me. Often."

"Were you—in love with her?"

"Love! That's another of those expensive words that wind up on the cut-rate counter. But I'll tell you this about Gilly. The papers have been having a Roman holiday with her reputation. But basically she was a good kid. She didn't lie, she didn't cheat, she gave fair exchange. If she'd had a little less beauty or a few more brains, she'd have been all right."

"It must have been a shock when you heard what she'd done."

"A shock?" He seemed to weigh the word. "Yes, I guess you'd call it a shock. I was surprised, I was sorry. I had no idea she was in that state of mind. But I was even sorrier that she didn't make it. The way I see it is, if you're that set on dying, you shouldn't have to go on living. Now the papers say she's getting better, that she'll probably recover. But God knows what kind of shape she'll be in. That could be a lot worse than a quick death."

"I heard," Selena said carefully, "that she might have been pregnant."

"What?" He stiffened with a suddenness that sent the green liqueur streaming across the table top. "There was nothing about that in the papers. Surely the doctor would— but he wouldn't necessarily tell the press. There may be some decency left." He put down his glass, stared at her intently. "Do you know that to be a fact? Did you hear it from somebody reliable or is it just a wild rumor?"

"I heard it—" a banging on the door cut short her answer.

"What the devil!" Jeff sprang to his feet.

"Hello, in there," a man's voice called. "Open up, here's the first of the big spenders." The banging began again.

Jeff strode to the door, flung it open.

"Framling! What in hell are you doing here?"

"Great to see you, boy, great!" The newcomer slapped him on the shoulder, ignored the inhospitable question. "The place is so dark that I thought, driving up, nobody else had gotten here yet." He looked at the blazing fire that was the only illumination. "Why don't you turn on some lights? You want people to think Lyndon lives here?" Chuckling at his own joke, he moved to switch on a lamp near the couch, became aware of Selena. "Well, hello!" He looked more closely. "It's Mrs. Mead, isn't it? I certainly didn't expect to see you here. Matter of fact," he turned to Jeff, "I didn't expect you either. You never have time for our little games."

"I don't know what your game is," Jeff said furiously. "But you can go and play it someplace else."

"Down, boy." Framling's good nature was undiminished. Selena recognized him as a congressman with whom she was slightly acquainted. "This is where the action is. Roll out the bankroll. It's high stakes tonight."

"You've got your dates mixed. There's no game here this evening."

"Then why are you here? What—" He shot a glance at Selena, gulped, said lamely, "Oh, I see." His confidence wavered. "Maybe I do have the wrong day. No, I don't! I wasn't home when the call came. My wife took the message and she never makes a mistake. Tonight at nine, she said. So I called Sam and Bert and they're on their way. Gosh, boy, I don't want to bust up your party." Again he looked toward Selena and reddened. "But I think you're the one who's mixed up."

"We won't argue that," Jeff grated. "You can just get back in your car and—"

The headlights of another car swung past the open doorway, stopping him.

"That must be Sam and Bert," said Framling.

"Go out and meet them," Jeff ordered. "Tell them you made a mistake and then all of you go home."

But it wasn't Sam and Bert. It was a general and a colonel. The general was an old friend of Selena's father.

"My dear." He bowed over her hand. "This is an unexpected pleasure."

He presented the colonel, whose pleasure was less evident.

"I didn't know this was a co-ed game," he muttered. "Is it going to be ladies' choice and everything wild?"

"She's not playing," Framling assured him. "There's been a little confusion. It seems we've crossed wires with a private party."

"Oh." The colonel looked from Selena to Jeff, nodded wisely. "Well, the house is big enough for everybody. Our crowd only needs the downstairs."

Selena had a sense of paralysis, of being unable to speak or move. The men kept coming. A senator and his assistant, two more congressmen, a member of the little Cabinet. All, on seeing her, made the jump quickly from astonishment to tolerant amusement.

"I—I'd like to go home." She forced the words through tight lips.

"Of course." Jeff went instantly for her coat. She snatched it from him, shaking off his attempt to help her into it.

She walked stiffly to the door, saying nothing, looking at no one. Neither she nor Jeff responded to the chorus of goodbyes. They were in the car by the time the laughter erupted in the room they'd left. She sat back in the corner, as far from him as possible.

He drove in silence till the house was far behind. Then he cleared his throat, said, "I—," coughed, began again, "It's a little hard to explain—"

"Don't try," she snapped. "Don't say anything. Just drive."

He accepted the dictum. Perhaps he was glad to. It was not till they reached her house that he attempted to speak again. She brushed past him, key in hand, to unlock her door and go inside without a word or a glance.

— — · — She hadn't yet taken off her coat when the phone summons came. No, she thought sinkingly, I won't go. I don't want to talk to Hugh. I've nothing to report. I can't tell him about that—that farce! But of course she moved obediently through the house and out to the garden.

He was in high good spirits, but her own mood was too leaden to hope that meant a favorable turn in the investigation. Which was as well, since he quickly showed a different cause for his cheerfulness.

"You're home early," he said as soon as they were inside.

"And without a scratch. Section Q takes care of its own."

"Section Q?" She looked at him blankly. "Did you have something to do with what happened tonight?"

"Of course." He looked down at her, smile broadening. "I gave it my personal attention."

"You mean those awful men—but they weren't—they couldn't be members of Section Q—not all of them."

"None of them. Tonight I assigned them as deputies, without their knowing it."

"That doesn't make sense. How could you get them to go out to Jeff's place if he didn't invite them?"

"Jeff's place?" His eyes widened in surprise. "Then you still don't know where you were?"

"I've a vague notion of the location," she said with dignity. "But I assume your men in the helicopter gave it to you exactly."

"They did indeed." He smiled again at the recollection. "You were hardly off the main highway before they tumbled to where you were heading. They passed the word downstairs and I began arranging the VIP parade."

"You knew about the place? It's not a secret hideaway?"

"Secret!" His smile broke to laughter. "It's about the best-known house in this area."

"If that's true, there was no point in my going there." She felt herself grow cold with fury. "Why did you insist on my finding out the location, if you already knew it? Was this some kind of giant practical joke?"

"Certainly not." With an effort he pulled his face to lines of sobriety. "You said Stone owned a place in the country. That sounded significant. Matter of fact, I chewed out two of my best men for not digging up a record of it. It didn't occur to me that what he had in mind was Harmony Hall." Again his lips trembled on the brink of a smile. "You've never heard of it? No, I suppose it isn't mentioned in your circles."

"What," she asked icily, "is Harmony Hall?"

"A house in the woods whose title is held by a front man chiefly distinguished by his obscurity and lack of occupation. Behind him stand a group of wheeler dealers who use it to help make laws and influence contracts."

"It doesn't belong to Jeff?"

"No, he borrowed it for the weekend. Making the place available to men who, for various reasons, want privacy is one of the ways the owners solidify their contacts. Evidently Stone thought the sordid background might stop you from going. He could be much more persuasive about a place of his own. As it turned out, he was right—though for the wrong reasons. I was the one he persuaded. If he'd said it was Harmony Hall, it would have saved us all a lot of trouble."

"Especially you. It must have been difficult to get so many poker players on the road."

"Only a few phone calls." He ignored the sarcasm. "The games at Harmony Hall are very popular. It's never hard to collect a crowd."

"I'm surprised they'd go such a distance when they could play the same game in town."

"Not quite the same game," he answered. "It's a haven for people who want to play together without being seen together. Large sums of money change hands, most of it in one direction. From the hosts to the guests. When a political jobholder shows up with an extra-large deposit, it's helpful to be able to refer to it truthfully as poker winnings. Some of them may not even know the game is fixed. They think they're smart or lucky. But it still makes them feel friendly toward the man who's pushing the chips their way. They'll pass his laws or buy his products so he can afford to lose to them again. I'm afraid tonight's play is going to be a disappointment. I only sent out the pigeons. There'll be nobody there to throw them corn."

"Won't they suspect that there was something odd about

the invitation, find out it didn't come from the people who run the place?"

"Probably not. They'll deal the cards, drink the liquor—which is always in plentiful supply—and think no more about it. Your friend Jeff is more likely to raise a ruckus. But an operation like that is impossible to pin down. All he'll learn is that somebody bonered. Or he may jump to your conclusion that it was one large hoax. Boy! I'd love to have seen his face when the first one walked in."

"If that's your idea of entertainment," she flared, "you'd have enjoyed mine even more. I'm afraid I have no sense of humor."

"I wasn't directing it for comedy. The objective was to get you out of there. On that score it succeeded."

"And sinking a ship drowns the rats, if you call that success. Go ahead, laugh. I'm sure it was screamingly funny. Like a George Abbott second act. Have you any conception of what it was like for me? Most of those men knew me, some of them are friends of my family, one of them lives across the alley. They came in and found me in what you now tell me is a notorious gambling den and—and love nest. The script was obvious. I'll probably be hearing from all of them next week, now that they know I'm available."

"You're exaggerating. You were there with Jeff Stone, who has at the moment no visible wife. It wasn't even very late. The worst they'll think is that you're his girl."

"This week's replacement for Gilly Conroy. That makes me feel much better."

"I'm sorry, Selena. I realize it was embarrassing for you."

"Embarrassing! I've never been so humiliated, so utterly ground into the dirt. The way they looked at me, then smiled at each other. And the way they laughed! But you're laughing too, aren't you? I'm proud that I could provide such general merriment."

"I had to act in a hurry," he defended. "It was the only way

I could think of to rescue you. Would you rather I'd set fire to the house?"

"Did it occur to you," she asked acidly, "that I might not want to be rescued?"

"No." He gave her a long look and the last vestige of mirth faded. "No, that didn't occur to me. The things you said the other night, the way you talked this morning gave me the impression that you found this assignment utterly abhorrent. I thought that any way I could get you back from the country in a hurry had to be a good way. Was I wrong?"

She pressed her lips tightly together to keep them from trembling, made no answer.

"All right." He lifted his shoulders, let them fall in an uncharacteristic show of weariness. "I should have found a more tactful method. I didn't take time to think of the spot it would put you in. But believe me, it's not that important. You'll feel better about it in the morning."

"I'll wake up laughing."

"You're upset," he said gently. "I shouldn't have come till you'd had time to get over it. We'll talk tomorrow." He started to leave, turned back. "Just one thing. Jeff Stone is suspected of treason. And the evidence is accumulating. Don't let yourself get emotionally involved."

"Don't let—!" Hysteria came close to the surface. "For days you've been pushing me at him, telling me to flirt with him, encourage him, go to bed with him!"

"I never—"

"No, you never gave that order. You only told me to do whatever was necessary. You don't have to draw diagrams. And all through it I was to be cool and indifferent and—and not emotionally involved. Maybe other people can manage that. Maybe you can. But I—" She took a deep breath and every word dropped like a stone. "I – am – not – a – machine."

He continued toward the door, not looking at her. "This may surprise you," he said. "Neither am I."

89

He had been gone for some time before she remembered the things she hadn't told him. What Jeff had said about Gilly. His late departure for Indianapolis. Above all—it came to her mind for the first time since dinner—the photographic fragment. She put out her hand to the phone, let it rest for a minute on the receiver, drew it back.

Let him wait, she decided. Let him wait!

CHAPTER FIVE

Sunday Morning

Coming home from church she found the red car parked in front of her house. Jeff sprang out as she approached, walked with her to the door.

"You don't want to see me, you don't want to talk to me, you don't want to have anything to do with me," he anticipated her rejection. "But neither do you want to create a scene on your front stoop. And I won't go away peaceably."

"As a candidate," she countered, "you have the most to lose by disturbing the peace. Have you forgotten that this block is filled with journalists and politicians?"

"I'm prepared to put on a show for all of them," he said. "You can take that as evidence of how much I need to talk to you, to straighten things out between us. I won't budge from this spot if Drew Pearson comes by hand-in-hand with Ev and Charlie. So shall we go inside and save your reputation?"

"What's left of it, you mean."

"Inside?" he said. "Please?"

But once in her living room, he was less ready-worded.

"If it's any satisfaction to you," he began, "I had a hard time shaving this morning. Couldn't bear to face myself in the mirror. And it's even more difficult to face you."

"Then why bother?" she asked coldly. "It would have been easier for both of us if you'd stayed home."

"I wanted to," he replied. "I'd like to wash the whole thing out, forget it, go on as if we'd never met."

"You'll have my full cooperation."

"Trouble is, I couldn't stay away. I had to see you. I don't expect, after last night, there's any future in it. But I had to come and at least say I'm sorry. If I could wipe it out, make it never have happened, I'd—I'd trade in all my ambitions. And that's not just campaign oratory."

"All right, I accept your apology. Now will you go?"

"And never come back?" He shook his head. "Not till I've made a better case for myself. Do you know where you were last night?"

"I do now. Apparently I'm the only adult in Washington who hadn't heard of Harmony Hall."

"You probably checked with your friend Beebee." He made a guess she didn't contradict. "She knows more than most adults. I should never have taken you there, I realize that now. My only excuse is that I thought you'd never learn the truth about the place and then where would the harm be? I put out the invitation on the spur of the moment, without even being sure that the house would be available. The next day I checked and was told I could have it."

"Along with a dozen other people."

"That's still a puzzle." He frowned. "I called the man in charge after I got home and he swears there was no game set up. He may have been lying in order not to admit that he fouled things up. Or somebody else may have made a mistake." He paused, his eyes lighting with a new thought. "Or perhaps it wasn't a mistake. I'm beginning to have a strong hunch as to what really happened."

"You—you are?"

"Travers. My secretary. It's just the thing his twisted little mind would plot out, if he thought he could get away with it."

"Oh no, I'm sure he didn't. It's not fair to put the blame on him."

"I'll soon be jealous of the fellow." He looked at her in

semiserious reproach. "The way you keep rushing to his defense. First, I shouldn't abandon him at the airport. Now, I'm not even to criticize him. What makes you so sure he's innocent?"

"I'm not sure at all; I don't know anything about him. Has he done anything like that before?"

"He wouldn't get two chances," he returned. "And to answer your other question, the one you didn't ask—no, he's never arranged a dinner party for me before. I had to turn it over to him because of being out of town. But he's well acquainted with the house. He's played in the poker games, so he knows who the players are and how to round up a tableful. The more I think about it, the more it points to him. I hope it gave him a hearty laugh. He won't be laughing soon again."

"But it seems so—so ridiculous—"

"Nothing's too ridiculous for Travers. Not if it would put me in hot water."

"If that's true, why did you hire him?"

"Because he's a damned hard worker and an efficient one. The fact that our personalities don't jibe is his problem, not mine. Whatever his feelings about me, I've been able to keep him strictly in line. Until now. But if he pulled that little trick last night—"

"I don't believe it." This time she kept from her tone the conviction that might suggest other knowledge. "It seems much more likely it was an error."

"I should be grateful to Travers." He smiled suddenly. "Pleading his cause has melted the icicles off your voice and I can talk better when I'm not shivering. So now I'll plead mine. Point one, I had no idea the evening would turn out the way it did. I'm sure you believe that. I don't have to offer proof. Second, it wasn't as bad as it seemed. I can imagine how you felt, but—"

"Oh no, you can't."

"Not entirely," he conceded. "But I know it was sheer hell. That's the end of it, though—or almost. Oh, there'll be a few snickers in bars and locker rooms and that's hell for you too, but it won't go far or last long. It isn't true that everyone knows about Harmony Hall. The knowledge is confined to a tight little circle and those who go there don't talk about it to those who don't. So the word will probably never reach the people you care most about. And the word itself is pretty limited. We had dinner there and left our dirty dishes for them. That's all they know for certain. That's all there is to know. Anyway, that part was out of my control. I was as much a victim as you. So I have just two things to answer for. I lied to you—because telling the truth would have killed my chances. And I took you to a place where you had no business being. To that I plead guilty with extenuating circumstances. I've a bad habit of putting all women into a single category. In the beginning it was 'way up on a pedestal. That's because my mother belonged there. It's from her that I got all my cornball ideas about truth and justice and sacrifice. She was a great soul. That's one belief I've never lost. Then I had a wife—and I transferred to her my illusions about the good and the true and the beautiful. Which is a heavy load for any woman to carry. Anyway, it was too heavy for her. I'm not saying anything about her that hasn't been, for a long time, common knowledge. After a few drinks she was an easy mark for any man who came along. So I opened my eyes and looked around and found a long line of women—other men's wives as well as free lancers—who were only too anxious to jump off the pedestal into the mire."

"Including me."

"No. Not you. That was my mistake, treating you as if you were like the others. I never really thought you were, not at any point. I was telling the truth when I said I hadn't expected to see you at the airport. And I was surprised again

95

when you didn't insist on coming straight back to town. Oh, I know I sounded confident, but it was all on the surface."

"Perhaps I'm the one who should apologize—for shattering your last illusion."

"No." His look was direct, unwavering. "My illusions about you are intact. Otherwise I wouldn't be here. I don't think it's just my ego telling me that, for you, last night was precedent-setting. I'm not asking you to make that kind of exception again. All I want is a fresh start, a slate washed clean, a chance to"—he paused and his smile verged on wistfulness—"to come courting."

"That's not possible," she answered honestly. "Last night happened. There's no way of forgetting, wiping it out. I don't see how, after that, there could ever be anything but unease between us." Suddenly, for the first time in the conversation, she remembered Section Q. She had been talking as if her feelings mattered, as if the decision to see him or not to see him rested with her alone. Now she was recalled to the true situation, the fact that her assignment was not concluded. She went on more equivocally, "But I—I realize it was as much my fault as yours. I'll think about it, that's the best I can say."

"Good enough!" He was on his feet, drawing her after him. "That's all I ask, more than I deserve. Now I'll clear out so you can start thinking. And I won't come back till your memory's had time to grow a little dim. Then maybe I won't be such a sharp reminder of the worst night of your life."

"Thank you." She squirmed inwardly at her own hypocrisy. "Perhaps all I need is a better perspective."

"The condemned man got a last-minute reprieve and lived happily ever after." His sigh of relief was exaggerated but genuine. "There's just one thing—" He paused, went on with reluctance. "I'd better get this last reminder over with and then we won't have to bring it up again, ever. You said something last night that's been nagging at me ever since. About Gilly's being pregnant. Did that have a solid base?"

"No, it was only a rumor. I was waiting in a senator's office and a girl who used to work with her was there. She said Gilly wasn't the type to commit suicide. The only thing she could think of that might make her do it was—that. You might call it an uneducated guess."

"I see." His eyes for several seconds were distant. Then he brought them back to her, made a circular, erasing motion with his hand. "Subject closed. I'll phone you in a day or two. Meantime—" He held up two crossed fingers.

His departure left her in a maelstrom of emotion. She was glad, in a way, that the next move was up to Section Q. Would Hugh tell her to go on seeing him or call off her part in the investigation? And if the latter, would she be relieved or disappointed? Jeff had been very convincing, seemed entirely sincere. Yet politicians are actors and an appearance of sincerity is their major asset. She was herself playing a role, leading him on for a hidden motive. He could dissemble as well as she. It was then that she began to wonder whether his entire performance, all his compliments and pleading, had been designed as smokescreen to lead up to and cover his final question. Had his visit had only one cause—to discover the source and soundness of her statement about Gilly?

For new light on that she had only a short wait. She was still in the doorway when—with a promptness that, lacking her knowledge of Section Q's efficiency, might have seemed magic—Hugh came loping along from the opposite corner. He stopped for a word with the man next door who was washing his car, included her in the greeting. To his casual "How's everything?" she answered, "Fine, except for minor annoyances. Like my percolator blowing fuses. Do you know anything about electricity?"

"Not much, but I'll take a look at it." He came toward her. "Probably a short circuit."

"I'll alert the fire department," the neighbor volunteered. "If you turn Picasso Jr. loose on your wiring, the whole block will go up in smoke."

"A Philistine," Hugh told Selena. "Never mind, we'll perk him a cup of hot coffee to eat his words with."

In the den he looked at her quizzically. "From the leap the congressman made over the side of his car, I deduce he'd just played a reconciliation scene. Is it a general amnesty? Am I covered?"

"I'm under orders," she reminded. "I'm not free to break with him until the assignment ends."

"My own petard," he admitted. "At least you're under the same compulsion to go on speaking to me. Very well." He became briskly businesslike. "What have you to tell me?"

"First, there's this." She handed him the piece of blue paper from the darkroom, went on to describe the circumstances of its discovery.

"Hm-m." He examined it with care. "I don't know what it's part of, but somebody will. So there's a photo lab at Harmony Hall. That's interesting. Photography can be a useful hobby for blackmailers. Especially in a place where they can snap their guests in a variety of compromising tableaux. We haven't paid much attention to that house. We know it's used for lobbying and salesmanship. Now we'll take a closer look." He pulled out his wallet, tucked the paper inside. "You did good work, picking this up. It makes your going out there exceedingly worth while, even though it didn't serve its original purpose. Anything else?"

"He talked about his trip, said he was late leaving Washington. He claimed a phone call from a constituent held him up till he missed his plane. The result was he didn't get to the banquet hall until dinner was over and the speechmaking under way. Perhaps you could check with the Air Force—he went to Indianapolis in one of their planes—and find out what time he actually left here."

"You think that might incriminate him?"

"I don't know. Probably it won't amount to anything. But it occurred to me that the real cause of the delay might have been that he had to meet the man who tried to kill Gilly."

"I'm reassured." Hugh smiled faintly. "After our talk last night I was afraid you might be inclined to hold back evidence against him."

"Oh no!" Shock turned at once to indignation. "How can you suggest such a thing? Do you think, just because women are used to make men turn traitor, that it can work in reverse, that I would— No! you couldn't possibly think that!"

"I couldn't possibly," he agreed. "Don't talk nonsense, Selena. All I meant was that your personal feelings might persuade you that some suspicious circumstances—little things like his unpunctuality in Indianapolis—had no significance, were not worth mentioning."

"And was it?" she demanded.

"Actually, no. We know all about the phone call. It was legitimate. My men followed him to the airport, saw him miss the plane by ten minutes, were in on the difficulties he had arranging another flight. The fact is, Stone doesn't crack an egg without our knowing it. We've had a tail on him since this thing began. If he had any open-air meetings, we'd be the first to know."

"Of course." She was deflated. "I should have realized that."

"But your job is to report the evidence, not judge it. And your passing this on lays my last doubt that he might be winning you to his side. Oh, I know," he added hastily, "it's a doubt I should never have harbored. Don't get the idea, though, that our ruling out the possibility of Stone's being 'John Smith' is a point in his favor. We're not dealing with a one-man show. Far from it. This is a well-organized group

99

and what Gilly knows is a danger to the whole operation. Even if the idea of having her killed originated with the congressman, he wouldn't be the man to hire the executioner. They'd send a go-between with the right knowledge and contacts."

"How sure are you," she asked, "of Jeff's involvement?"

"Right now, we're sure of nothing. We're still groping in the dark."

"But last night you spoke of accumulating evidence."

"In the heat of the moment," he admitted, "I played it a little strong. The nearest thing we have to evidence is a document that is known to have passed through his hands last week. Yesterday one of our men who's planted on the route to Red China saw a copy on the desk of one of his contacts. Stone isn't the only one it could have come from, of course. But of all the people who have had that particular paper, he's the only one who is also a member of the Committee involved in this other investigation. In other words, we get a meeting of lines over his name. If it isn't coincidence, then it's a fix we can steer by. That's the only new lead. But data is building up in the old areas. His wife is applying thumbscrews for a heavy settlement and full custody of the daughter. It appears her interest in the girl isn't as great as her desire to hit out at her husband. Whether his motive is also dog-in-the-manger or more paternal in nature isn't clear, but he is determined to take her from her mother, whom no one could call a good influence. She's threatening to drag him into court with a series of scarlet charges. Even if they're false, they could finish him politically."

"What has that to do with his being a spy?"

"She can be bought. Our information is that a sufficiently large payment will not only keep her quiet but convince her that the child will be better off with her father. But it will take a lot of money. Far more than Stone can lay his hands on. Unless he's found a foreign source."

"So he needs money. Many people do. That doesn't make them traitors."

"Their names aren't on envelopes containing classified information found at the scene of an attempted murder. And they're not intimately involved with the murderee. That's another area in which evidence is increasing. There's no doubt that he and Gilly were having an affair."

"I know that. He said so last night. I dropped her name, as you told me to do."

"And his response?"

"He was annoyed at having her brought into our conversation, but no more than was natural under the circumstances. He called her a good kid, said he was sorry for her and wished she'd succeeded in dying, since that's what she wanted to do. I didn't get the impression there was any depth of feeling between them. He liked her, she was useful to him, that was all."

"Which is about what I'd expect him to tell you. It's not likely he'd launch into a declaration of grand passion for another woman."

"That may be so," she said, "but I believe him. I don't think he could have talked about her with such casualness if he seriously cared."

"All right, I'll trust your instinct. Even though it's on the bias."

"I'm aware that he'd try to be casual, no matter how he felt. But I don't think he'd succeed, not totally. I wasn't just hearing his words. I was watching his face, listening to his voice, and it all added up to a too-bad-so-what attitude. He's not that good an actor. I know, because when I mentioned the possibility of her being pregnant, he wasn't at all casual."

"You brought that up, even though you knew it wasn't true?"

"I thought his reaction might be interesting. And it was. He was upset, disturbed, intense. All the emotions that the other talk about her didn't even start to arouse. And it was still on his mind today. It may be the real reason he came to see me. Of course he said it was to apologize, to be friends again. But just before he left he asked me where I'd heard that about Gilly. He hadn't been able to pin it down last night because right after I said it the card players began arriving."

"And what answer did you give him?"

"The truth. That it was a theory of one of her friends."

"You've just thrown light on a minor enigma," he told her. "Stone phoned the hospital late last night, talked to Gilly's nurse, wanted to get in touch with her doctor. The nurse asked for his name, said she'd have the doctor call him back, but he refused to give it. He put the nurse through a set of questions about her condition, didn't directly ask about pregnancy, but that may be what he was trying to draw out. Up to now he's stayed clear of any contact with the hospital. Evidently you pushed him into risking a phone call. I wonder what makes it so vital to him."

"That's not hard to understand. If he thinks she's going to have a child and he's the father—"

"But he could assume that, whatever her condition a week ago, jumping off a bridge would put it in the past tense. The explanation can't be that simple. Next time you see him, try to get a clearer line."

"There's to be a next time?"

"That's optional."

"Nothing's optional," she returned. "If there are still things for me to find out, I'll have to go on seeing him."

"I hope you're as unwilling as you sound."

"One other thing." She changed the subject. "He thinks his secretary may have started the word that there was a poker game last night. Can you do something about that?"

"What kind of something?"

"Make it clear somehow that he wasn't responsible."

"Why should we? It's a perfect answer. Maybe we can start the players thinking the same way, in case they're puzzled by the absence of the hosts and their bankroll."

"But the poor man may lose his job. That would be very unjust."

"It's a small injustice, compared to the work we're doing."

"There's no such thing as small injustice," she retorted. "Jeff has nothing to go on except that they dislike each other, they're on very bad terms and Mr. Travers knows about the house and the poker games. But it's a charge he can't disprove and it may get him fired."

"So you want me to call the congressman and explain that last night's debacle was arranged by Section Q as part of our investigation of his possibly treasonable activities."

"Of course not. But there must be some way you can clear the secretary without—"

She never finished the sentence. A low buzzing from Hugh's watch sent him at once to her phone. He dialed, said "Pierce here," listened, asked "She did? What time?" listened again, said "Who knows about it?" nodded satisfaction at the answer and concluded, "I'll be right there. Hold the pose."

He hung up, his face in grim lines. Selena scarcely needed to ask the question.

"Is she—?"

"Yes," he told her. "Gilly's dead."

CHAPTER SIX

Sunday Afternoon

She tried to persuade him to take her to the hospital.

"I told you I had a plan, something that might bring the opposition out of hiding. Now's the time to put it into effect."

"I've a hunch as to what your plan is," he answered. "Nothing doing."

"You can at least listen before you say no. I'll describe it on the way over."

"You know better than that. Our arriving together at Gilly's hospital would set off a blare of trumpets. I go in with a load of linens and you don't look like a laundryman's assistant."

"No, I look like a visitor to a sick friend. So I'll meet you there. How many people have heard about her death?"

"Those in the room with her, you and I."

"Nobody outside Section Q?"

"Not yet. They won't move till I get there. Then we'll have to work out some kind of announcement."

"First," she begged, "hear me. After the announcement is made, it will be too late. You're in a bad spot. What little chance there was of her coming to and saying something useful is gone for good. Once the other side knows she's dead, they can relax. All I ask is that you listen to me. Then if you say no, I won't argue."

"I'll say no," he assured her, "but—O.K., you can make your

106

pitch. When you get to the hospital, say you're visiting John Quinn. They'll send you to the room next to Gilly's and I'll find you there."

The man using the name "John Quinn" was an ambulatory patient.

"Got a strange malady that puzzles the doctor," he told Selena while she waited in his room for Hugh. "He's been keeping me here for observation while I keep that door under observation." He nodded toward the bathroom that connected his room with Gilly's.

"Is she—still in there?"

"Yes." He nodded somberly. "We've been expecting her heart to stop beating, but we were hoping for a few more days. This will take the heat off them just when it might begin to burn."

"Maybe not." Selena took quick advantage of the opportunity to gain an ally. "If you could hold back word of her death, make them believe she was conscious again, able to talk, almost ready to leave the hospital—would that help?"

"Would it help!" His voice rose but as quickly fell again. "No, I guess not. There's a limit to how far you can run a bluff. They bit on our hook by sending out a killer Friday night, but that bait's stale. It will take something stronger than another 'getting better' bulletin to raise them to the surface. And with the girl dead—"

"What I'm thinking of is much stronger than a bulletin," Selena said. "Suppose we show them a picture of Gilly sitting up, talking, walking even?"

"A picture of Gilly—" He looked at her strangely. "You know a way to raise the dead?"

"I know a way to make her appear alive. Not just a story that they may not believe but proof positive that she's come out of the coma, made a near miraculous recovery."

"If you could do that!" he said fervently. "If only that were possible, we'd have them on the skillet."

"That's why I'm here. Because I know I can. Have you seen Gilly?"

"No, I'm the outside man. By an odd coincidence, we have the same doctor, but he's the only link between her room and mine. Except for that door which was locked when I moved in and, in the view of the hospital authorities, has never been unlocked. But what does my seeing her have to do with your scheme?"

"Only that I thought you might— Oh, here you are." She broke off at the entrance of Hugh, accompanied by a woman in nurse's uniform and a man carrying a doctor's black bag.

"Might as well get it over with," the doctor was saying. "Put out the death notice in routine fashion, call in the undertaker. Delay won't get us anything but funny looks from the reporters."

"That's your department," Hugh said wearily. "From here on, you can handle it like any other death. There'll have to be some phrase like 'sudden relapse' to cover those favorable forecasts you've been making, but otherwise the truth will do it."

"You promised me," Selena cut in, "that you'd listen to me before you took any action."

"I'm about to listen," he said. "But while I do the doctor can be thinking up his statement."

"Maybe no statement will be necessary. I've told him about my plan." She indicated Quinn. "He thinks it's a splendid idea."

"You do?" Hugh looked sternly at the pseudo-patient. "Aren't you stepping outside your jurisdiction?"

"I never heard any plan," he denied. "We were just talking about what a bad break we got with the girl's dying so soon."

"That's it," Selena said eagerly. "And he agreed that it

would be very helpful if we could convince everyone that she's still alive. Not only alive but almost well."

"All right." Hugh spoke with resignation. "I've been expecting this. Let's get it over with so we can all go back to work. You think you're a ringer for Gilly."

"You told me yourself I looked like her."

"She does!" the nurse exclaimed. "She really does! There's an amazing resemblance."

"That's right," the doctor seconded. "The high forehead, the oval line from cheek to jaw. Yes, the skull would be very similar. Maybe a little taller, but not much. More slender."

"But Gilly would lose weight in a coma," Selena said. "That would be expected."

"True," the doctor agreed. "Intravenous feeding isn't conducive to chubbiness."

"All right, you've made your point," Hugh said. "You look alike. So?"

"That's it," Selena said. "I take Gilly's place. The doctor issues a statement that she's out of the coma and able to talk again. The papers can publish a picture of me, fully conscious. You can even say that she's going to have a press conference. That ought to scare the other side."

"It will scare them all right. What do you think they'll do about it?"

"Everything in their power to stop my talking. And it's too important to take chances on a hired man botching the job again. This ought to bring out one of their own people."

"Say!" Quinn put in. "She may have something there. It could be just the gimmick we need."

"It would be a great gimmick," Hugh said contemptuously, "if we were dealing with morons. That's the only type that would swallow such a story. Here's a girl who was mixed up with a spy ring, got pushed off a bridge. Finally she wakes up, poses for a picture, says 'I want to talk to the press' and then shuts her mouth again till the story of her consciousness gets into wide circulation. They know damn well she'd talk first to a cop and next to an intelligence agent. We'd have her whole story and put the girl under wraps long before the news of her recovery hit the street. Trying to shut her up then would be locking the hangar behind a stolen plane, even if they thought they could get through our guard. We could have said Gilly was conscious two days ago, if we didn't know their only hope was to stop her before she came to, not after. So that's that. Satisfied, Selena? Can we get on with our business?"

"I'm not a moron either," she retorted. "I realize that they won't risk an attack if they think she's already told what she knows. But she was seriously injured. She's been in a coma. There was a concussion, perhaps brain damage. I don't know how it would be stated medically. That's the doctor's responsibility. But the substance of the report would be that she's almost well physically, able to walk, talk, eat, perform all the normal functions. But her memory is defective, especially in relation to recent events. She remembers nothing at all about last Tuesday. She can't understand why she's in a hospital, was totally baffled when told that she jumped from Calvert Bridge. She has no recollection of being on the bridge or any reason for jumping."

"Circumscribed amnesia." The doctor nodded professionally. "A frequent follow-up of psychological stress. A certain period of time, which contains unwelcome material, is repressed, though all that goes before and all that follows is remembered. In the patient's mind it is as if a particular traumatic situation had never occurred, because all memory of it is blocked. The blank areas can cover persons, places and events."

"And could you predict," Selena asked him, "as a medical probability, that with the passage of time, memory might return in its entirety?"

"Absolutely. The disassociative state is often temporary.

Memory sometimes returns little by little, filling in the blank patches over a period of days or weeks. Or it can come back altogether, in an instant. In any given case it would be impossible to predict whether recovery would be gradual or instantaneous."

"Perfect!" said Quinn with enthusiasm. "A diagnosis like that would put our fish on a barbed hook."

"It might be worth trying," Hugh said more cautiously. "It means getting the body out of there in a hurry, without anyone knowing."

"That's no problem," the doctor said.

"I know. It's only a matter of logistics, working out a time-table. Give us until 5 P.M., then notify the local press that she's come to. Say you'll let in reporters and photographers at 7 for a brief interview."

"We'll bandage her head." The nurse nodded toward Selena. "A high thick bandage. That will add credibility to the picture and minimize any flaws in the resemblance."

"The interview will be a cinch," Quinn said. "She just has to keep saying, 'I don't know, I can't remember' to every question. With an occasional dramatic pause as if something was flashing through her mind before she could catch hold of it."

"You should write television scripts," Hugh told him.

"Hey!" He was unquelled by the sarcasm. "That's what we need—TV. We don't want to wait till they see the morning papers. Night's the best time for them to strike."

"Good thinking." Hugh gave him ungrudging credit. "We'll have a film of the interview on the 11 P.M. news, every channel."

"She looks like Gilly," the nurse pointed out. "But will she sound like her? None of us ever heard the girl talk."

"I believe I can." Selena dropped into a low-pitched drawl. "Ah do believe ah cay-un."

111

"You go too far," Quinn said. "Nobody has that many grits on her tongue."

"Marilee has," Selena told him. "And Gilly's boy friends were always mistaking their voices." She turned to Hugh. "Did you get the record of her Lady Macbeth?"

"We borrowed it, copied it on tape and put it back before Marilee had time to miss it." He pulled a spool of celluloid from his pocket and showed it to her. "We'll bring in a player and you can listen to it while we're setting the stage. Since you won't have much to say, the accent shouldn't be a problem."

"Keep it soft and weak," the doctor suggested, "as if the words were coming with difficulty. They'll attribute any change to the brain injury. It isn't as if they had any reason to suspect a substitution. They'll assume it's Gilly until proved otherwise."

"They'll assume it's Gilly," Quinn agreed. "But will they swallow the amnesia story whole? You had me all steamed up for a minute," he told Selena, "but my second thoughts are sober. Like the man said, this begins to sound like a television script. Just the plot we'd dream up if the girl suddenly got conscious and spilled the whole story. It would be our way of getting them to come to us. Their only response to your 'I don't remembers' may be 'like hell she doesn't.' Maybe it's not such a great idea, after all."

"I never thought it was," Hugh retorted. "But while we're waiting for a great idea, we might as well check out the mediocre ones. My guess is, this will leave us right where we started. But as far as I can see, there's no risk involved. We try it, it fails; no profit, no loss. You'll do your ten-minute act before the cameras, Selena, and be safely home long before the film hits the picture tubes. All the rest of us have to lose is another night's sleep. So we might as well try for that one chance in a hundred that they'll bite on it. Don't get your hopes up, though. I'll be very much surprised if morning finds us with even a minnow in our nets."

"So will I," Selena said.

"So will you!" He looked at her, astonished. "You mean to say all this hard sell was for a plan you don't even have faith in yourself?"

"Oh, I have faith in the plan," she answered. "I just don't expect tonight's part of it to get any results. That's only the beginning."

"What do you mean, the beginning?"

"Tonight we establish beyond doubt that she's alive and conscious. They see her awake, hear her say a few words, watch her struggling to remember. They wonder how much she's told the authorities, whether her loss of memory is real or pretended. They suspect a trap and they won't walk into it. The most they'll do tonight is send another hired gunman who doesn't know his employer's name, which will be of no help to us. But I don't think they'll even do that. As you said, there's no point in killing her if she's already talked. And if she has, if she's given names and places, they'll expect our side to make the next move. So they'll wait and they'll worry. That's all that will happen tonight. Then tomorrow the second part of my plan will go into effect."

"Tomorrow?" Hugh eyed her warily. "The second part?"

"Gilly will go home. Everything here is strange. She's unhappy about being in a hospital, she wants out. Physically, she's all right. Mentally, too, except for the blank patches in her memory. And that's more likely to come back in familiar surroundings. Maybe you can roll out the television cameras again to show her leaving the hospital, arriving back at her own apartment. Then the opposition may begin to believe what they see. Because if you knew she was involved with a spy ring and could identify the others in it, you probably wouldn't let her go home again."

"You're damn right we wouldn't!" Hugh said. "A few men

113

can guard a hospital room. Setting up security for an apartment building is much more complicated. If she really had come to and started to talk, our first act would have been to get her out of here and into a place where nobody but ourselves would know where she was."

"Good," Selena said. "They'll be aware that that's standard procedure. You wouldn't expose a valuable witness to danger. So her being in her own apartment will go a long way toward making them believe the amnesia story."

"And after we show the homecoming films, what then?"

"I stay in her apartment," she answered, "and wait. I think I'll soon have some interesting company."

"Oh no, you don't!" Hugh exploded. "I've heard some crazy schemes, but this tops them all. We'll go along with your little playlet tonight because it's harmless. But tomorrow we announce Gilly's death and that will be the end of it."

"They might go for the apartment gag," Quinn said. "It looks a lot more free and easy than keeping her in a hospital."

"And it's just as free and easy as it looks," Hugh snapped. "We can't provide a hundred per cent security in that building and you know it."

"There's no such thing as a hundred per cent security," Quinn answered. "The whole country found that out last November. But we can provide ninety-five per cent." He stopped, noting Hugh's expression, and added quickly, "I guess, in this case, that's not enough. Here's an option. We can take pictures of her going home, but she doesn't have to stay there. We get her away by the back door, then stake out the place."

"All that trouble," Hugh said, "to collect another hired gun. That's what we'll get out of it. If anything."

"I think we'll get more than that," Selena argued. "As long as Gilly was still in a coma, killing her was all that was necessary. But after she's been conscious for twenty-four hours, they're going to need to know whom she's talked to and what she's said. And the only way they can find that out is by coming themselves."

"She's right," Quinn said. "A talking Gilly presents them with an entirely different problem. They'll weigh the chance that it's a trap against their need to know and it may tip the scales on our side."

"There's another item going for us," the nurse offered. "We don't know the circumstances of her being thrown off the bridge or who did it. It doesn't have to prove that she's broken with the men we're trying to catch. Perhaps they may still hope to use her. And in that case someone might show up at her apartment to talk business."

"I agree," the doctor said. "Her being conscious will change the picture completely. A big fish might swim into that net."

"And that's why I have to be there," Selena followed up. "It's not enough to stake out the place and catch the fish. There's no certainty that, after you catch him, you can make him talk. But if I'm there—well guarded, of course, but with him not knowing there's anyone there but me—he may say something useful. At least—" She repeated Hugh's phrase. "It's worth trying."

"We've wasted enough time!" Hugh was on his feet, his face hard. "Get your statement ready," he told the doctor. "We're announcing at once that Gilly's dead."

"But—" Selena began.

"I promised to listen to you. I kept my promise. Your whole plan's haywire and I want no part of it."

"But you agreed that it might be worth while to say she was conscious and bring in the press. You—"

"I said I'd go along with it tonight," he came back, "because it would do no harm. But we all know that we'd just be treading water. And now that I've heard your second act,

I'm ruling out the whole project. I'm laying no foundation for any such insanity."

"It might work," she said softly. "Don't you believe it could draw out—somebody important?"

"Yes, I believe that." He looked at her directly. "I also believe that you could get killed. We can guard the building, throw a cordon around the apartment you're in and keep everybody out. But your plan entails letting one of them through, giving him a chance to get close to you, talk to you, when he thinks you're alone. There's no way we can guarantee your safety in a setup like that."

"I know that," she answered. "I also know that in Section Q all agents are expendable."

She looked at him. Quinn, the doctor, the nurse looked at him. She was thinking of Simon, who had proved to be so very expendable. The others were thinking of themselves. They all took risks, moved unhesitatingly into situations where their lives might be forfeit. Why was she, their eyes questioned, an exception?

Hugh's eyes made a circuit of their faces and he had no answer.

"All right, Doc," he said heavily. "Start working on the amnesia statement. Fill it with technical terms. We'll set up the press conference. Maybe it will bring us a prize catch tonight. If not—" He looked again at Selena, pulled his shoulders straight. "I'll make that decision tomorrow."

CHAPTER SEVEN

Sunday Night

Out, damned spot! Out, I say! One, two, why then 'tis time to do it. Hell is murky! Fie, my lord, fie! A soldier and afraid? What need we fear who knows it, when none can call our power to account? Yet who would have thought the old man to have had so much blood in him?

The soft accent of the Deep South was incongruous accompaniment to the words of Macbeth's homicidal queen. Selena, sitting in Quinn's room as the tape unreeled, tuned her ear to the accent, shut out the words. But their import of death and damnation was underlined by the knowledge that the voice speaking them was forever silenced. Listening became even more eerie after Hugh came in to say, "We're about to take the body away. I think you should see her first. It may help you act the part."

She went with him to stand beside the long operating-room cart onto which the corpse had been transferred, holding herself rigid as the sheet was pulled back to reveal the head still swathed in bandages, the bruised and discolored face. Hugh watched her impassively, but she suspected that his primary motive in bringing her here was not to aid her impersonation but to plant this sight in her memory as deterrent to her plans for tomorrow. It was, she admitted, a clever stratagem, since the horror stayed in her mind while she listened, again and again, to the elocutionary flourishes of the murdered girl proclaiming that "all the perfumes of Arabia will not sweeten this little hand."

Between playings she rehearsed with Quinn, altering the voice she had learned from Marilee to reproduce the slightly more husky quality of Gilly.

"Ah don' remembah. Ah jes' don' remembah," would be her principal line and she said it over and over till Quinn declared that he couldn't tell record from imitation.

"If the going gets rough," he advised, "Yell 'out, damned spot!' That should clear the room in a hurry."

Too soon it was time to go into the other room, undress and put on a white hospital gown. The nurse expertly wound the bandages and, thickly turbaned, Selena took her place in the recently vacated bed. The news of her consciousness had already been a radio bulletin. All that remained was to add auditory and visual proof.

Promptly at seven the doctor opened the door to the men with microphones, cameras and notebooks. His crisp Section Q manner had been displaced by that of a genial public-relations-conscious practitioner.

"Now remember, boys," he admonished, "this is a very weak little lady. Don't press her too hard. The minute she shows signs of tiring, I'll have to ask you to leave."

"Shades of Barnum!" a reporter on the far side of the room muttered to a colleague. "The lengths some of these medicos go to get round that advertising-is-unethical rule. This johnnie's been calling the city room every hour on the hour to tell the world what a great job he's doing. And now—" He indicated the assemblage. "This circus! He'll get his phiz in front of a camera if it kills the patient."

The first questions were easy, dealing with her physical condition, how she was feeling.

"I'm just fine," she told them in the voice of Gilly. "I'm all right." She touched the bandage. "My head aches—just a little—not bad. And he says—" she looked gratefully at the doctor, "in a little bit—the ache will go away."

"It will," he assured her. "Soon you'll be perfectly well."

"And then I can go home." She managed a tremulous smile. "Back to my own place. Oh, they've been most kind to me here." She looked from doctor to nurse. "I declare they have. But it's not like being in my own place."

Quickly the questions moved to harder ground, to the subject of Calvert Bridge and she began her chorus of don't knows, don't remembers.

"They tell me," she said incredulously, "that I—I fell off that bridge. But I don't remember one thing about it. Why would I—" Her voice rose plaintively. "Why ever would I be on a bridge in the middle of the night?"

"Were you unhappy?" a newsman asked. "Did you have any reason to want to die?"

"Oh no!" She stared at him apprehensively. "I don't want to die. I swear I don't want to die!"

"Careful, boys." The doctor lifted a warning hand. "Don't push."

"I keep thinking about that bridge," she said. "Since they told me, I keep thinking and trying to remember." She screwed her eyes tight shut in concentration, opened them again to stare fixedly at a corner of the room. She spoke in a slow, weighted voice, Gilly's conception of the sleepwalking Lady Macbeth. "There was a bridge—yes, there was— and I was—there was some—" Again she closed her eyes, opened them, shook her head, said sadly, "No, I just don't remember."

"Don't force it." The doctor patted her hand. "It will all come back to you if you take it easy, let it happen by itself." He spoke pontifically to the others. "This is a standard case of traumatic disassociation. Her memory may come back suddenly, all in one piece. Or it may be a gradual return. Don't worry, my dear." Again he was paternal. "You will remember everything very soon."

"I will," she said positively. "I know I will as soon as I'm in my own place. How can I remember anything when I'm where it's all so strange? This high bed—those white walls—everybody tiptoeing around on rubber shoes. They showed me a mirror and I didn't even know myself. No make-up. My hair all cut short." She touched her hand to her cheeks, raised them to the bandage. "And this great gob of white wrapping. I declare I look a fright. I just got to go home, doctor. I'll never get well here."

"All in good time."

"Tomorrow?" she begged. "You said it might be I could go home tomorrow."

"If you rest and don't try too hard to think and get rid of those headaches, then we'll see."

"I was up today," she told them proudly. "I walked."

"Indeed she did." The doctor's pride equalled hers. "She took a few steps and sat in a chair." He beamed down at her. "This is my little medical miracle. Luckily, no bones were broken. And now that her mind is clearing— Who knows, maybe we will let her go back to her own apartment tomorrow, since her heart is set on it."

"If only I could remember!" She frowned, pressed her palm against her forehead. "There's something—somebody—"

"Easy," the doctor cautioned. "Let it come when it's ready. And now, boys." He was briskly efficient. "We must let the little lady rest. You've had time enough."

He followed them out to complete the case history. Selena sank back against the pillows, as exhausted from the ordeal as if she were in truth only five days removed from a fall from a bridge.

"Next stop Hollywood," the nurse said. "If I hadn't seen her go out of here under a sheet, I'd have believed it myself."

Hugh, when he joined them a few minutes later, was more restrained.

"Good show," he said. "That agonized frown and those on-again, off-again flashes of memory may draw blood. There's a bare chance it will scare them into moving tonight. But leave the I-want-to-go-home bit to Garbo. You may have sold the doctor and the newsboys, but my resistance stays high. Now get out of that bandage and into your own clothes. I've a man waiting in Quinn's room to drive you home."

Alone in her own house, the evening dragged on interminably. At eleven o'clock she turned on television, watched with chilled fascination the scene in the hospital room, tried to imagine other rooms where other watchers, as deeply—but differently—concerned as she, would view the performance and perhaps be driven by it to desperate action. She shut off the set in the middle of a report of the Elizabeth Taylor-Richard Burton marriage and went slowly up to her room, though sleep seemed a remote prospect. She undressed, got into bed, picked up a magazine at random from the bedside table.

How long would it be—her thoughts superimposed themselves on the printed page. Suppose they sent someone at once to the hospital, one of their own people, who knew the answers and could be made to give them, how long would it be before she'd hear? Would Hugh call her, send her word? She stared at the phone, willing it to ring. For all her impassioned arguments in favor of taking Gilly's place again tomorrow, she shrank from the thought, longed for release from the necessity. If only tonight would bring the rats from their holes, close the case without her further intervention!

The phone didn't ring. Instead, so suddenly that she dropped the magazine, a horn blast broke the night's stillness. It came from behind her house: – – Instinctively she waited for the short and long that would complete the signal, though noises loud enough to rouse the block were hardly in character for Section Q. There was, however, no short blast, only a prolonged trumpeting that seemed destined never to stop. She slid her feet into slippers, pulled on a robe, hurried downstairs. The horn was silent by the time she reached her back door, but when she stepped into the garden, there was a new noise as someone shook the iron gate with frenzied violence.

For an instant fear clutched her throat. So close had been her identification with Gilly that she believed in that moment that Gilly's killer stood at her gate. At once she realized the impossibility. It was only when she was disguised as Gilly, possessed—presumably—of Gilly's knowledge, that she was in any danger. In her own person she was a threat to no one. Even if, by some incredible chance, her role as Gilly's double were suspected, they'd still have no cause to endanger themselves by coming after her. Another angry rattle speeded her steps to the garden wall. She pushed a button to light the lamp that stood over it, revealing the face of Congressman Stone.

"Jeff!" She was startled by the dark anger of his expression. "What on earth! Why have you come by the back way? Why have you come at all?"

"Open up!" Again he shook the gate. "Let me in."

She released the chain, stepped back. He entered, slammed the gate behind him.

"Isn't this the usual entryway," he snarled, "for your after midnight visitors?"

"I—I don't understand."

"Of course you don't! You're so innocent!"

She was dismayed by the malevolence of his tone, the belligerence of his stance, but all she said was, "Let's go indoors before we wake up all the neighbors."

"Sorry," he sneered. "I should have come more quietly.

It will never do to let them know you have another back-door suitor. By all means, let's get out of the alley and into the house."

She made no answer till they were in the living room.

"Now," she demanded, "what is this all about? Have you been drinking? Or have you lost your mind?"

"I had," he said. "But I found it again. With the help of a kind friend. Oh, you took me in completely. Selena the untouchable, the blue-blooded aristocrat, the goddess on the golden pedestal. I came here this morning and groveled, crawled on my belly, because I'd had the presumption to treat you like a woman. Ha!" His laugh was harsh, gritty. "A great joke on me, wasn't it? How you must have smiled behind my back. Well, let's laugh together now that we're both in on the joke."

"I'm waiting," she said quietly, "for you to explain."

"Explain? Oh no. The explanation should come from you. If you have one. But I see what puzzles you. You had me so utterly hoodwinked, so under your spell that you can't understand how I could come to my senses so quickly. Believe me, it took a real jolt to do it. I was in hell last night thinking of the spot I'd put you in, how you must hate me for it. And this morning when you were so magnanimous, when it looked as if I'd talked you into giving me another chance—my God! It was like lighting a candle in a mine! This afternoon I ran into one of the men who found us there last night and I thought I could make a start on clearing your name. I told him I'd driven you out there to show you the house, we'd had dinner and were about to start back when they came, that any ideas he might have gotten were way out of line, you weren't that kind of girl, and so on and on and on. He laughed in my face."

"He—laughed?" She'd been drawn taut, waiting for him to tell her that he'd discovered her counterespionage assignment, knew her reason for seeing him. Now she went limp, her bewilderment genuine.

"That's right, laughed. Loud and dirty. 'You don't have to tell me what kind of a girl Selena is,' he said. 'I live right across the alley from her and I see what goes on in her house. If my wife wasn't such a hawkeye, I'd try to get in on it myself.' That's what he told me. God! I was ready to hit him."

"I don't understand," she said. "Nothing goes on here. Why would anyone make up a story like that?"

"Was he wrong?" He looked at her, a little less certain, then shook his head. "No, he had his facts too straight."

"What facts?"

"Did you really think you were getting away with it, that nobody knew except you and your Bohemian boy friend?"

"Bohemian?" She was struck with sudden knowledge of where he was leading, weakened by her total inability to cope with it. "What exactly did he tell you?"

"He said that sometimes, late at night, when he can't sleep, he goes out to his back garden for a cigar. A bad break for you that his wife won't let him smoke in the house. And several times he's heard that artist fellow—what's his name? Hugh Pierce—come padding down the alley with his dog as camouflage. And you've been waiting inside your gate to let him in." He looked at her with renewed contempt. "The first time was a few days after your husband died. What answer have you to that?"

"Hugh's an old friend of my family. He and my brother were at school together. He's almost like an older brother himself. My husband and he saw a lot of each other. So when Simon died he came often—as a friend, a neighbor—to offer help, to give me comfort, to let me know there was someone nearby I could lean on. Is that so strange?"

"Not strange at all," he jeered. "Except that neighbors visit by daylight, family friends enter by the front door. The kind of comfort that sneaks up the alley in dead of night isn't brotherly. Think of a better story."

"I have no better story."

"And he does come, just as your neighbor says? You admit it?"

"I admit it." She drew herself straight, made her eyes meet his.

"I see." It was his eyes that dropped. The anger was gone now, his voice drained of emotion. "I came here to hear you deny it. I knew in my heart it was true. But I wanted you to say he was lying, that you'd had trouble over garages or garbage or whatever neighbors fight about and he was slandering you to get even. But you admit it. It's all true."

"It—it's not the way it sounds."

"No? What way is it? I suppose you're crazy about his dog, can't sleep until you've given him a good-night pat."

"I can't explain," she said. "I can only tell you that—that what you think isn't true."

"Why him?" he exploded. "A sloppy down-at-the-heels paint dauber who never pulled his weight in any boat. Why didn't you at least pick somebody you wouldn't have to be ashamed of?"

"I'm not ashamed of him!" For a minute her anger matched his. "And I'm not ashamed of anything I've done. Whatever I do, it's my own business. I owe you no explanation."

"You're right. You owe me nothing! You didn't fool me, I fooled myself, I wanted to be fooled. I tell myself I'm wise now, cured of all my young ideas, that I see the world the way it is. But I have this weakness, I keep hoping I'll be proved wrong, find out that everybody isn't rotten, that there really are two kinds of women. When you came along I told myself you were real, the princess quality was more than skin deep. And when you went to the country with me, I still told myself, This isn't her line, she's unwilling, she's

126

here in spite of herself. And coming home, with you on that high plane of injured dignity, I believed even more strongly. I congratulate you on a brilliant performance. God! when I remember my abjection this morning, how I licked the dust at your feet! Well, I'm not at your feet now." He stepped forward, put out his hands to grasp her upper arms so tightly that his fingers bit deep into her flesh.

"No." She tried unsuccessfully to pull away. "Don't."

"The blinders are off. I see you as you are. But don't worry." His lips curved in a mirthless smile. "I like what I see. And now that I've stopped building a wall around you with fairy-tale notions, we can be very close friends."

He pulled her nearer as she struggled for release.

"Go on," he said. "Fight. Make it interesting. But don't keep it up too long. I may lose patience."

He leaned down, closed his mouth over hers. One arm was behind her back, his other hand fumbled with the top button of her robe. She put up a hand to force his head back and, using all her strength, twisted free.

"I came through the back door this time," he reminded her. "That gives me certain privileges."

"Get out," she said. "Get out and don't ever come back."

"You do it so well," he said. "You almost make me believe it."

"Get out."

"Oh no." He shook his head. "You owe me something and I'm here to collect. Nobody makes a fool out of Jeff Stone and comes off scot free."

She stepped around the couch, faced him over its back. Despite her anger she had a strong sense of absurdity. Is this how it's going to end, she asked herself, a chase round my living room? Last night George Abbott. Mack Sennett tonight. And some place out in the dark were the men from Q assigned to trail the congressman. Had they notified Hugh that he was in her house? Was he about to send another posse? All the situation needed was for Hugh himself to walk in and complete the triangle. No, she realized soberly, whatever the men outside were doing, they weren't notifying Hugh. She'd let Jeff in herself, they'd have seen that. They were no doubt patiently waiting for him to emerge so they could pick up the trail again. Hugh was at the hospital, keeping vigil. She wasn't his business tonight.

"Please!" she said to the man on the other side of the couch. "Please go."

"You sound real," he told her. "I wish you were. I wish I still believed in you. But I know now you're like all the others. A phony." He took a step forward, she took a step back. "Knowing that has advantages too." They continued to move clockwise around the couch. A half-smile flickered across his lips. "You're working your way toward a dead end, you know. Then we can quit playing games, get on with the business of the evening."

She looked behind her, saw that he was right and stopped moving. Instead she flung at him, with seeming irrelevance, "I saw your friend Gilly tonight."

"Saw Gilly?" It stopped him. He stood still and stared at her. "You saw Gilly?"

"On television. The broadcast at eleven. Didn't you see it?"

"No. I haven't been home." He looked at her, his eyes dulled. He seemed all at once without energy. "Since this afternoon, since he told me—about you—I've been driving, out in the country, all around, I don't know where, just driving. I didn't turn on the radio. I didn't even have anything to eat. I just kept going, trying to adjust to the idea that you're not somebody special, no different from—from Gilly— or anybody else. Why was Gilly on television? Has she come to?"

"Yes." Selena took a deep breath. The chase was over, but she felt no satisfaction. "Reporters were interviewing her.

She looked and sounded fine. She said she was anxious to get out of the hospital, go home. And the doctor said perhaps she could go tomorrow."

"She's all right then." He thrust his hand through his hair, leaving it in disarray. "I'm glad." He looked at her for several seconds as if at a stranger. "I don't get it," he said at last. "You're half come-on, half go-away. I could figure that when I thought you had scruples. But now that I know you haven't, this tightrope act doesn't make sense. What's your problem?"

"I do have scruples," she said, "even if you don't believe me."

"How can I believe you when I know— Oh, the hell with it! I'm going home." His smile was sardonic. "You've broken the mood."

When he was gone she went once more to bed. She thought again of Hugh and the other watchers at the hospital, wondered if there had been as yet any developments. But most of her thoughts were of Congressman Stone. Her arms were sore from the pressure of his fingers, her lips bruised from the roughness of his kiss. But what rang in her ears were his words, "Driving. Just driving." And her resentment was vanquished by her memory of the anguish in his voice, the pain in his eyes.

CHAPTER EIGHT

Monday Morning

She dreamed again of Simon. This time it was not a happy dream of being together in closeness and comfort. Instead she was seeking him in an alley, long and dark and seemingly endless, an alley like the one in which an assassin's knife had struck him down. She saw him ahead of her, a shadowy figure, just out of reach. She began to run, in the way of dreams, faster and faster but always in the same place. Then with a spurt of speed, her lungs almost bursting, she caught up with him, called his name. He turned and it wasn't Simon. It was a stranger, yet she had a vague sense of recognition. He raised his hand above her head and a blade flashed in it. Beyond him was another dark, running figure. That one, she knew, was Simon. She tried to cry out, failed, tried again.

"Simon!" The sound of her voice, strained, hollow, brought her to consciousness. It took her a minute to realize that she was safe in her own room, her own bed and she felt the usual release of awakening from nightmare. But it lasted only an instant before the events of yesterday came flooding back to swamp her in the worse-than-nightmare promise of the day that lay ahead. She shut her eyes against the pale light of early morning, willing time to stand still, the day never to advance. It took physical force to get out of bed, dress, ready herself for whatever she had to do.

Neither the morning paper nor the radio brought any solace. Both had, so far as Gilly was concerned, only last night's news. She was conscious, she wanted to go home. But that didn't prove that there hadn't been activity at the hospital. Whatever happened, Section Q would not inform the press. She tried to make herself believe that there had been developments favorable to their cause, ruling out need to go forward with her plan. That she had not heard was no reason to think there was nothing to hear. They'd be too busy to notify her. She had, in security terms, no need to know. She was in a suspended state of awaiting instructions. All she had to do was stay in place, keep herself available until someone came to tell her what to do. She'd made her recommendation, offered herself. The responsibility was no longer hers. And she knew with certainty that if she remained quiescent, nothing would happen. Hugh would not send for her, would not implement her plan. She could rest satisfied in the knowledge that she'd formed it, proposed it —and been freed of it by someone else's decision. The only way to set it in motion was to confront him again in the presence of his associates and force his hand through their silent suasion.

No, she thought firmly, I've done my part. I tried. But I don't want to do it. He won't let me do it. Let it rest. But while thinking that she was on her way to the door. She opened it, stepped outside. The sun was bright on her doorstep, yet she had the feeling that she was once more walking into the dark alley of her dream.

It was far too early for visiting hours at the hospital, so she chose a side entrance and followed two chattering young women—nurses or nurse's aides—trying to look, like them, on business bent. She rode the service elevator to what had been Gilly's floor, managed to evoke neither notice nor questions till she was again in Quinn's room.

"An early bird," he greeted her. "But no worm."

"Didn't anyone come?"

"No fish, no rat, no other animal species."

"Then we've made no progress."

"None." It was Hugh, coming in from the next room, who answered.

"A quiet night," Quinn said. "I even managed to catch some sleep."

It was a statement that Hugh, to judge by his haggard appearance, could not echo. "Why are you here?" he asked her.

She stood straighter, met his eyes steadily. "Reporting for duty," she said.

"Go home," he ordered. "If I want you, I'll send for you."

Instead she moved to seat herself on the foot of Quinn's bed.

"We could still try the stakeout," Quinn suggested. "The way we talked about it yesterday. Make them believe she's in the apartment, but get her away and set a tight guard."

"Don't be childish," Hugh growled. "They won't walk into a trap. We gave them a chance to do that last night."

"A hospital's not a home," Quinn said irrepressibly. "Maybe they don't like this antiseptic atmosphere. I don't myself."

"You can check out any time," Hugh told him. "We've no further use for this room."

"Why not give the apartment a try?" Quinn urged. "Strictly from desperation. It isn't as if we had anything else on the agenda."

"That's not true," Hugh said. "The Harmony Hall lead may work." He turned to Selena. "I got a reading on that scrap you found in the copying machine. It matches a corner of a map that was shown to the Joint Committee. It must have been taken out and photographed."

"Do you think Jeff—Congressman Stone took it there?"

"He may have passed it over, but he didn't make the copy. That diagram was brought to the Committee room with a batch of other material by a high-ranking Pentagon official. He began his testimony shortly before the Monday meeting ended, finished it on Tuesday morning. There was nothing missing from the file when he took it back. That means that if the map was siphoned off through the Committee, it had to be taken on Monday, returned early Tuesday. We've checked the congressman's Monday movements. He didn't leave the Capitol till time to catch the shuttle plane to New York for an eight o'clock rally. He spent the night there, shuttled back the next morning in time for the hearings. He could have met somebody before he left, given him the map and gotten it back from him Tuesday morning. But it wasn't possible for him to go to Harmony Hall himself."

"Then what I found neither proves him guilty nor clears him. It seems to me it just makes everything more confused. So why do you call it a lead?"

"Because," Hugh said patiently, "it provides a direct link between Harmony Hall and the spy ring. It indicates the photo lab was set up for more important purposes than simple domestic blackmail, that the owners have gotten into deeper waters than the influence racket. We've agents checking everybody who uses the house or has any connection with it."

"A vast network," Quinn put in. "Separating the red sheep from the black is going to take time. Which is something we don't have. It's nearly a week since they found the girl under the bridge. That map holds the key to our basic strategy. If it's on its way through the channels to China, it may already be too late."

"I know how long it's been," Hugh said icily, "and how fast time is running out. Do you have a way to speed up our processes?"

"Not me." Quinn looked toward Selena. "But maybe she has. It will take days for the boys to unravel the Harmony

Hall skein. We might as well kill part of the waiting time by playing games in Gilly's apartment."

"I told you—" Hugh began, was interrupted by the nurse's entrance. "Has Doc got his statement ready?" he asked her.

"He's polishing the phrases." She adjusted the cuffs on her uniform. "Trying to salvage as much as he can of his medical good name. What a relief to get out of that hospital gown. The knots are lumpy. No wonder patients are always complaining. Oh, hello." She saw Selena. "That bed's had quite a turnover. I replaced you, spent the night in it."

"As a decoy?" Selena asked.

"Yes. In the dark we didn't need a look-alike, just a female form. So I was elected."

"You might have been killed."

"Might have," she agreed cheerfully, "if your act had stirred up the natives. Unluckily, it didn't. Maybe it didn't fool them."

"One person it fooled," Hugh said, "was your friend Marilee."

"How do you know that?"

"The man from *Candid Confessions* went back to get more data for his article on Gilly. Somehow it led to an invitation to dinner and they finished the evening in front of her television set. He didn't leave until after the eleven o'clock news. We were anxious to get an immediate reaction to the substitution from a close friend. You passed inspection with an A-minus. Her only adverse comment was that you sounded a little hoarse, which she took as the natural effect of being unable to talk for five days. We can assume that the people toward whom we beamed it didn't know her nearly as well as Marilee did. So if they have doubts, they probably aren't on the matter of identification but on the amnesia story. But the whole question is moot, since we don't— Well, Doc?" He let the sentence drop as the doctor joined them. "It's about time. You got it?"

"Look it over." The other man's face was glum as he gave Hugh a sheet of paper. "It's fortunate Section Q keeps me supplied with special cases. Burying my medical miracles is a poor way to build a private practice."

"Is that—" Selena looked in consternation at the paper in Hugh's hand. "That's not a death announcement, is it?"

"Oh you're back in the picture." Noticing her, the doctor's glumness lightened. "Then maybe we won't use my statement. At least not right away."

"Not today." Selena spoke before Hugh could answer. "You've got to let me try," she pleaded. "It may not be much of a chance, but it's a chance, and this is too vital to let one day slip away without grasping even the flimsiest of straws. I have a clear idea of the danger. You don't have to remind me. I may be killed—" she turned toward the nurse, "just as she might have been killed last night." She didn't add, Where's the difference? But the question hung in the atmosphere and Hugh was forced to acknowledge it.

"It's not the same," he told them. "The risk last night was minimal. We had to have the bed occupied to keep up the fiction of Gilly's being still alive. But she wasn't impersonating Gilly, she wasn't going to hold any conversations. The only thing we were expecting last night was another man with a gun or a knife and we were set up to stop him before he got past her door. If someone had come with plans to talk, he'd talk to us, not her. What you want to do is totally different. We could put you in Gilly's apartment. We could provide you with reasonable protection, what Quinn calls 95 per cent, against a man who came only to kill. But that's not what you're aiming for. The nub of your plan, the whole point of moving from the hospital to Gilly's apartment, is to attract someone who needs to get information before he shoots. We can throw up a circle to keep him from getting to you. But once we let him through, once he's close enough to talk, we lose the advantage. Your chance of being attacked last night," he told the nurse, "was less than one in a hundred. This other situation reverses the odds."

"Statistics!" Selena said scornfully. "Did you figure the odds against Simon?" She rushed on before he could speak. "If you want to juggle numbers, I'll join the game. Put me in Gilly's apartment and three things can happen. The first is—nothing. I'll sit there for twenty-four hours and no one will come. You'll gain nothing. I'll be in no danger. The second possibility is that they'll send another gunman. I don't think they will. If all they wanted now was Gilly's death, speed would be of first importance and they'd have acted last night. Still, it's a possibility and one against which you say you can furnish nearly perfect protection. So the profit and risk are balanced. Then there's number three. And that's the one you're afraid of."

She paused, gave him a steady glance, saw him flinch from the word. Tension heightened as they all looked at Hugh, waited for her to continue.

"Someone may come, a man in authority, to talk to Gilly, ask questions, use persuasion and, when the conversation is ended, kill her. If that happens, I'll keep him talking as long as I can. You'll be listening. So you'll learn everything he has to say to Gilly, plus what you can make him say to you. You'll open a hole through your circle to let him in, but you'll close it before he gets out. I'm not risking my life for a will-o'-the-wisp. If we get no results, I'll be alive tomorrow. If the plan is effective, if you're unable to save me, you'll have him. However it goes, the gain will equal the loss. And the loss will be mine only. The gain will be the nation's security. You can't ask for better odds than that."

"We can cut the odds," Quinn suggested. "Once he's through, we can move in close, be ready to jump the second he shows signs that the talking part is finished, the action about to begin."

"We're dealing with a brain," Hugh said. "He won't start

talking unless he's convinced she's alone. If our men are far enough away for him to believe that, they won't be near enough to move before it's too late."

"If he's a brain," Quinn insisted, "he'll be practical. It's the morons and maniacs who are the most dangerous. There'll be a talk-back on our listening machine and we can let him know he's surrounded, that he can't escape. He'll have sense enough to see that it won't help his case to add a witnessed murder to the unproved charges against him. I vote we give it a try."

"My vote is the only one that counts," Hugh snapped. "And I don't like anything about it."

"Why not?" Selena pressed him. "If you thought nothing would come of it, you wouldn't be so opposed. You do believe someone will come. Someone clever and wily and resourceful. Don't you?"

"It's possible," he answered, "that it will pull out someone who's smarter than I am, someone even Quinn can't out-guess. All our planning may not be a match for him."

"Then he'd be very worth capturing," she said quietly. "We've got to try. I've got to try."

He looked at her, seemed about to argue, and for a moment it was as if they were alone in the room. Then the presence of the others was heavy around them, with all three voting yes. Nobody spoke until Hugh, his shoulders dropping in a shrug of acceptance, crumpled the death notice in his hand.

"All right," he said, "we'll take a chance." The weakness was at once past and he began barking orders. "Take a crew to the apartment," he told Quinn, "and make it safe. Ninety-nine per cent safe. Tell the boys who wire it for sound that the mechanism has to be as invisible as if they were bugging Khrushchev's bedroom. We want to be able to hear a whisper from any point. You go to the apartment too," he said to the nurse. "Yours is a visible errand. You can be seen coming and going, so ask the superintendent for the key. You're getting clothes for Gilly to wear home."

"Something not too fitted," Selena suggested, "since we're not quite the same size."

"She probably wore them tight," the nurse said. "So they ought to be just right on you."

"You'll need a new statement, Doc," Hugh went on. "Back to the miraculous-recovery line. Tell the press Gilly will go home late this afternoon, but the exact time isn't set yet. It won't be, until we know how long Quinn's preparations will take. Say you'll give them an hour's notice so they can come and take pictures. We'll aim for a spot on the six o'clock news." He turned to Quinn, who was pulling trousers on over his pajamas. "All right, get going."

The absent Quinn had a number of visitors that day. One brought the scrapbooks Marilee had lent to *Candid Confessions*. Selena spread them out on the dead girl's empty bed, settled down to steep herself in Gilly's life history. Other men came and went, getting their orders, leaving to carry them out. The doctor worked on his new statement and, when it was written, he and Hugh left together. The nurse came back with a green jumper and yellow blouse.

"I also scooped up all the cosmetics that were on her dresser," she reported. "She'd have been sure to ask for them."

Selena put on the jumper and found the nurse correct in her estimate of fit. Then she experimented with make-up till her face was a close approximation of the newspaper photo that had been her first encounter with Gilly. These activities kept her busy, kept her, thankfully, from too much thinking. It was midafternoon when Hugh came back again. His entrance was the nurse's cue to leave.

"I've done all I can," he said tiredly, "taken every precaution that can be taken without scaring them away. But it's

not enough. It never can be enough. What you said this
morning is true. Either we're wasting our time and nothing
will come of this—or you're in grave danger. I can't take you
out of it now, it's gone too far. You put pressure on me this
morning, you did it deliberately, I know. And now I'm committed. But you can still change your mind, take yourself out.
We can go through with this up to the point where you enter
the apartment. Then you go away again, fast, and we stay
on guard. That may net us something."

"But the chances are far greater if I'm there. Aren't they?"

"Of our catching someone, yes. But I'm thinking of your
chances of staying alive."

"If everyone who ever worked for Q and all the other
branches of Security had concentrated on staying alive, the
other side would be 'way ahead. You need this information,
Hugh. You need to close this leak, to catch these men. Can
you honestly tell me that's not worth one man's life?"

"It doesn't have to be yours, Selena."

"Today it does. No one else can do this job. I have peculiar
qualifications."

"They think I've gone soft." He gestured toward Quinn's
room, the site of the debate. "That I was holding off from this
because of the way I feel about you. And I gave in because I
couldn't entirely deny it. But I also have a more acceptable
reason. I put Simon on the job that led to his death. That's
enough to ask of one family. I have no right to put your life
on the line too."

"I'm putting it there, not you. And Simon's being dead
makes it easier."

"My God, Selena, you don't mean—you don't want—"

"Of course not. I want to live. Life isn't as great as it was a
year ago, but it's worth going on with. And I expect to go on.
I have faith in your precautions. I have faith in myself. We're
both committed, Hugh. Why wear ourselves out arguing?"

"You're right," he said. "There's other ground we should cover."

A head appeared in the doorway, summoning him to the next room. Left alone, she thought of possible "other ground." A last will and testament? She sloughed off the thought. She would, no matter what Hugh said, what he feared, come through this alive. Neither did she have to deal with the complications that her murder, while in the role of Gilly, would create for Section Q. Simon had been knifed in a back alley, but his body had been found in a wrecked auto on Memorial Bridge. Section Q had managed that, they could cope with a surplus of corpses in Gilly's clothing.

She shivered involuntarily, pulled away from the idea's gruesome fascination. That was certainly not ground to cover with Hugh. What then? Congressman Stone. She should, she realized, have told him about last night. But what was there to say? That Jeff had come—belligerently, insultingly—to charge that she and Hugh were lovers, that their affair was the talk of the neighborhood. She felt color creep up her throat and cheeks, partly at the memory of Jeff's charges, even more at the notion of repeating them to Hugh. I can't possibly tell him, she thought, I'd rather die—and felt a shock at the current truth in the cliché. Yet, considering it with care, she saw no reason to tell him. She would only embarrass herself to no purpose. Jeff's visit had been entirely personal. Nothing he said could have any significance for Section Q. No, she told herself, there's no need to bring it up at all. Eased by the decision, she went back to the scrapbooks, tried to merge her identity with that of the girl who had grown up as the belle of a small Southern town.

In a few minutes Hugh was back. He shut the door with a small click, stood with his back against it. His eyes fixed on her with new severity.

"Why didn't you tell me," he asked sharply, "that you had a caller in the middle of the night? What did he want?"

She stiffened at his tone, his look, felt a sudden, irrational anger.

"Can't you guess?" she demanded. "I'm a light woman, with men coming and going at all hours. Everybody in the neighborhood knows that. What do you think he wanted?"

He was rocked by her vehemence. He blinked, continued more mildly, "That's what I'm waiting for you to tell me. What do you mean, light woman? Have you dropped into character as Gilly? If so, you forgot the accent."

"I don't need an accent. I'm speaking as me, Selena Mead, the girl with the shredded reputation."

"Oh Lord! Are we back on the Harmony Hall deal? I told you I was sorry, I made a bad arrangement. We haven't time to play that record again. What I want to hear now is about last night. I've been bird-dogging it around so much today, the reports have been slow catching up with me. And the boys on Stone's tail didn't stamp theirs urgent because they knew I saw you early this morning. They took for granted that you'd filled me in. Why didn't you?"

"Now you have their report." She ignored the question. "What did they say?"

"That he led them on a wild ride through the countryside, going nowhere at top speed and wound up in your alley. Quit stalling, Selena. I want to know why he was there—and why I didn't get the information hours ago, without having to drag it out of you piece by piece."

"I didn't tell you," she said through tight lips, "because it had nothing whatever to do with this case. But since you insist, I'll tell you now. He came because he'd heard about you."

"What!" His eyes went wide with surprise, then narrowed. "What had he heard about me?"

"One of my good neighbors told him that you're in the habit of slipping in my back gate after the rest of the block is in bed. He sits across the alley and smokes a cigar and

143

watches you arrive. Apparently the cigar never lasts long enough for him to see your exit."

"Oh." He looked at her in silence for several seconds and, since there didn't seem to be much else to say, repeated, "Oh." He crossed to the chair beside the bed, sat down and studied the floor pattern with apparently great interest. "I suppose I should have foreseen something like this. That connecting alley was just too easy. And when I used it to meet with Simon, nobody paid any attention. I didn't stop to think that your situation made things different. Thoughtless of me. When this is over, we'll have to work out a new means of contact."

"Why bother?" she asked bitterly. "If your visits stop now, the word will go round that we've quarreled. It will only give them something new to gossip about."

"What can I say?" He spread his palms helplessly. "I goofed, I'm sorry." There was sincere concern in his voice, but she sensed beneath it a tremor of amusement. "The Victorians had a word for it. I've compromised you. They also had a required solution. Maybe I'll take that up with you some time." He glanced round the stark hospital room. "Under more appropriate circumstances. Right now we're talking about Stone. You say he came to see you because of what he'd been told about us. What business was it of his?"

"He was in a rage, really beside himself. He accused me of giving him a false impression, making him believe that I was—was better than I am. He said I'd held him off with a pretense of virtue while all the time I was carrying on a—an affair with you. He went on and on about it. I tried to explain that you were a very old family friend, a classmate of my brother's, that you only came out of sympathy."

"That should have stopped him." In her preoccupation, she didn't notice the slight edge to Hugh's voice. "Anyone can tell that I'm the avuncular type."

"He wouldn't listen." She spoke with a desolation that made him look at her with new perception. "I couldn't make him believe me. Then he—" She cut herself short. "That's the whole story."

"Is it? Was that all he did—talk?"

"He—" She stopped, bit her lip. "That's all. And as you can see, none of it is relevant to my assignment."

"Agreed," he said. "And I don't suppose the part you've censored out is relevant either. But next time I think I'll tell the boys not to wait in the alley."

"There won't be a next time," she said. "I won't be seeing him again."

There was an instant silence as both were struck with the thought that tonight could bring, for her, an end to all "next times." In thinking that, she realized that she had, after all, a final testament.

"In case," she said, "anything goes wrong tonight, would you do one thing for me? Find a way to let Jeff know that what he thinks about me isn't true."

He accepted without protest the implications of her "in case."

"I'll do what I can," he said, "to clear your name all down the line. But I can't guarantee results. In this work reputations have to be expendable too."

"I'm well aware of that. Simon's on record as having died in a one-car crash. Most of our friends believe—they don't say so to me, but I know they think it—that he was speeding, reckless, maybe drunk."

"Doc had a fine reputation," Hugh countered, "before he joined Q. He's one of the best brain surgeons in the country and he has a high degree of professional pride. But he's been parading before the press as a publicity-grabbing quack. And I—since we're being personal—I don't get much satisfaction out of being the Charlie Chaplin of the paintbrush. But that's how our job gets done."

"I'm not worried about my reputation. Not now. The neighbors can think what they like. The whole city can think what it likes. I just want Jeff to know that I was honest with him."

"Why is that so important?" Hugh's voice cooled. "He has a very tarnished halo. What right has he to expect more of you?"

"No right at all. But he's had a lot of rafts shot from under him in his life. And what he learned about me may have sunk the last one. If possible, I'd like to give it back to him. I said he was in a rage last night and he was, but underneath he was terribly hurt."

"Great God, Selena! We're trailing this man as a spy and you're crying over his delicate sensibilities!"

"He's not a spy. I'm sure he's not."

"You're not sure of anything."

"Do you know something about him you haven't told me?" she demanded. "You said you'd checked his movements last Monday. What about Tuesday night?"

"He stayed late at his office, getting his weekend speeches written and mimeographed for release to the press. He had his whole staff working with him, so there are five people who can swear to his being there till 11 P.M. But the crucial time is midnight. And we've no way of finding out whether he went directly back to his hotel or detoured by way of Gilly's apartment and Calvert Bridge."

"Then you're no more sure than I am."

"Granted. But until we are, the rule has to be, don't trust anyone, no matter how sad a spaniel he seems to be. Yes, what do you want?" The last words cracked angrily at Quinn, who stepped through the doorway.

"No offense, massuh suh." He put up a hand in mock expectation of a blow. "Just came to tell you everything's ready at the apartment. We've a listening post on the roof, guards above, below, behind, beyond." He glanced at Selena. "All that's left to do is put the bait on the hook."

"Good." Hugh consulted his watch. "For once everything's

synchronized. Doc told the cameras to line up on the front lawn at five sharp. That gives us forty minutes. Tell Jean we're ready for her to wind the bandage." Quinn went out, was immediately back with the nurse as Hugh explained, "It was so becoming we thought you should wear it again today. Also—" He drew a metal sphere from his pocket, gave it to the nurse. "This will be buried inside. The devices on the roof will pick up the smallest sound from Gilly's apartment, but we have to allow for mechanical error. That's our insurance policy. A recorder. All you have to do is press here." He indicated a point over her left ear. "That will start it taping every word that's spoken."

"But it won't be connected to the roof?"

"No, it doesn't transmit, only records. We'll have to wait till we unwind the bandage to hear its story."

"You haven't introduced me," Quinn said. "Ah'm yo' lil ol' brothuh that yo' hain't seen for yars and yars. Yassuh, ah come all the way to Yankeeland to look aftuh mah baby sistuh till she husseff agin."

Selena looked at him, unsure whether he was serious or clowning.

"That's right," Hugh said. "He's going with you, as your brother."

"But I'm supposed to be alone. That's the whole point."

"The point is," Hugh corrected, "to make your leaving here seem normal and logical and unsuspicious. Miracle or not, it would be odd to send a girl just out of a coma and with only half a memory to live alone. In fact, an appearance of being alone would almost certainly clue them to the fact that you had a hidden escort. But an obvious escort can make them think that, aside from him, you're alone."

"Logic," Quinn murmured. "Beautiful logic."

"Taking a nurse with you would supply the logic but no protection. Quinn can supply both."

"I'm the fastest tackle," he boasted, "this side of all-America."

"But if he's with me, they won't come."

"If they have business with Gilly," Hugh said, "seeing Quinn won't stop them. They'll be sure they can deal with him. Anyone who could be put off by a hayseed brother no brighter than he looks doesn't belong in this trade."

"Thankee, suh," Quinn said. "Thankee kindly."

"Gilly has—had a brother. Surely he doesn't, he couldn't look like him."

"No, we're not that loaded with coincidences. But the only one of Gilly's friends in this town who knew her brother was Marilee. Her recollection of him will be pretty dim. And Quinn's not going to get close to the cameras or do any talking. That Uncle Tom act is strictly for your entertainment in the event you have no other company tonight."

"What if the real brother hears that he's supposed to be visiting her?"

"He's on a ship in the South Pacific. And Gilly's fame is strictly local. If, by an off-chance, somebody who knows the brother sees the show, he's not going to be in touch with the crowd that interests us. By the time fact catches up with fiction, it will be long past the time of its mattering to us. Believe me, Selena, we've covered all the angles." Hugh paused, went on more slowly. "At least, I hope we have. There's always the chance of human error. And for that—" His eyes lingered on the miniature recorder the nurse was covering with white strands of bandage. "For that we've no insurance."

CHAPTER NINE

Monday Evening

She sat with Quinn and watched the six o'clock news on Gilly's television set. She saw herself—lipsticked and mascaraed beyond recognition—smile coquettishly and wave at the reporters. The head bandage barely showed its edges beneath a gaily patterned scarf. A man held a microphone to her lips, asked about her memory.

"I'll be fine," she said bravely in Gilly's voice. "I just know I'll be fine as soon as I'm in my own place. My head doesn't ache any more and I keep getting so close to remembering everything. Then it slips away because I look around me and feel so strange. But when I'm home I'll be myself again, I declare I will."

The doctor stepped in with his usual officiousness to ward off further questions and take her arm as she walked to the waiting cab. Television had recorded, too, her arrival at her own apartment. Quinn's face, bespectacled and owlish above a sailor's uniform, flashed quickly past as he held the door for her entrance.

"My film debut," he complained at the brevity of his stay on the screen. "And no chance to mug at the camera."

When the show ended there was nothing to do. Gilly's apartment was on the top floor. Hugh was on the roof, right overhead, with the listening crew, equipped to hear, to talk, to direct citywide operations. It gave her an odd feeling to know that every word she spoke, every movement she made would carry at once to his ears. Perhaps it also inhibited Quinn, for after a few feeble attempts at humor he too fell to silence.

It was broken by the telephone's sharp pealing. Tense in every muscle, she walked over to lift the receiver with a hand she could not keep from trembling, held still for several seconds before she could trust her voice in the single word " hello." The result was anticlimax. Marilee's voice, bubbling with pleasure and curiosity, flowed to her ear.

"Honey, I saw you on the TV last night and again today and I was just so thrilled I had to call and say how wonderful it is that you're well again. Do you feel all right, really all right?"

"Honey, I'm fine. It's just so wonderful to be home again."

"And it's so lovely that Eugene has come to be with you. Honestly, I never would have recognized him. Of course, how could I? He was just a boy when he went away and now he's a handsome man. You tell him I said that, won't you?"

"I surely will, he'll be pleased. And I want you to come and visit while he's here. But not tonight. What with moving out of the hospital and all, I'm pretty tired."

"Oh no, not tonight," Marilee agreed readily. "I've a date with this perfectly marvelous boy. He works for a magazine and he's writing a story about you. That's how I met him. You don't mind, do you?" Her voice grew anxious. "My telling him how we were children together and all?"

"Oh no, honey. I know anything you say about me will be kindly."

"It is, for true. Anyway, this is a perfectly darling boy and I know he'll write nice things about you. We were in this swanky cocktail place and he had them turn on the TV and there you were. I was so excited and he said why didn't I call and tell you how happy I was about your being back home. That's the kind of sweet, thoughtful boy he is. Someday I want you to meet him." She hesitated, added quickly, "But

151

not tonight. Honey, I have to run now. He's waiting to take me to dinner. I just wanted you to know how glad I am that you're well."

"I do thank you, Marilee. I appreciate your calling."

She put down the phone, turned accusingly to Quinn. "You knew she was going to call."

"It seemed a good idea," he admitted, "to try a dry run under pressure."

"How many other dry runs will there be?"

"None. The next event will be totally unscheduled."

On his last word the phone rang again. She shot him a doubting glance but knew from his face that this was indeed not on the program. She let it ring twice in a deliberate effort at relaxation before she answered.

"Gilly? Is that you?"

"Yes, it's—" The shock of hearing Stone's voice, so out of context, made her almost forget her imitation. "This is Gilly. Who is it calling?"

"It's Jeff. I've got to see you. Right away."

"Jeff?" She made her voice vague, as if groping to remember. "Oh yes, Jeff. Honey, I'd love to see you, I surely would. Are you coming over now?"

"Not to your apartment. You've had so much publicity, you're a nine-day wonder. Your place must be surrounded with newshawks and I don't want to run into any of them."

"Oh no, Jeff, there's nobody here but me and my brother. If you come and visit me, he can go out for a while. He wants to see a movie anyway."

"There's probably a pad-and-pencil brigade sitting in your lobby waiting for a new lead. I don't intend to be it."

"You say you want to see me and then you say you won't come over. I don't understand you, Jeff."

"I want you to meet me. Away from your apartment, where we can be private."

"But Jeff, honey, I just got out of a hospital. I can't be running all over town. Why won't you come here?"

"I told you." He was impatient. "I don't want my name in the papers as your first visitor. You walked out of the hospital, you looked perfectly healthy. You can walk out of your apartment too. We'll go for a ride."

"Jeff, I think you're being silly. Why won't you come to my apartment?"

"Gilly, I told you. If you're too stupid to—" He broke off, spoke more gently. "What I'm asking is simple. I want to talk to you and I want to do it now. But I can't afford to have flashbulbs popping in my face while you're a Sunday-supplement sensation. All you have to do is walk out of your building and go half a block to the corner drugstore. Go in the front door and out the side. I'll be there with my car to pick you up in exactly forty minutes. If there are reporters on watch, say you're going to buy aspirin. They know you have headaches. Do you understand that?"

"I understand, but I don't—"

"The side door of the drugstore, forty minutes from now. You be there."

The phone went dead. Quinn withdrew his ear from the other side of the receiver. "A masterful type," he murmured. "And used to blind obedience from our girl Gilly."

"If he's so determined to talk to her," Selena wondered, "why won't he come here?"

"Could be for the reason he said. It would make a pretty headline. 'Party Girl Cheats Death to Entertain Congressman.' Or it could be for other reasons. Having to do with why we're gathered here tonight."

"There's only one way to find out." She looked at the clock. "He said forty minutes. I suppose I should allow ten minutes to get from here to the drugstore."

"Are you out of your mind, Selena?" Hugh's voice crackled

from a speaker concealed in a lamp base. "You're not seriously proposing to go out and meet him?"

"I must." She was surprised at the question. "You have the phone tapped, don't you? You heard what he said. He absolutely refused to come here."

"Then he'll have to get along without talking to you. You're not to leave that apartment tonight. Haven't you any sense at all? Don't you realize that his prime objective is to get you away from there, someplace alone with him, where you can't be encircled with guards?"

"You're assuming," she said, "that he's a traitor."

"Yes," Hugh answered, "I'm assuming that. Do you think all he has in mind is a romantic ride in the moonlight?"

"No," she said slowly. "I think what you think. That's why I have to go with him."

"You'll stay right where you are. I'll have him picked up at the drugstore. Now that he's tipped his hand by trying to arrange a rendezvous, we may be able to break him down."

"You never will," she said. "You can't make him talk. But he'll talk to Gilly. And I have the recorder in my bandage to get it all down."

"You'd get nothing down," Hugh came back, "except his astonishment at finding you in Gilly's clothing. How long do you think it would take him to tumble to your disguise? I'll give you the answer. Less than a minute. This man's no fool. He's known Gilly for a long time, known her intimately. And in the last few days, he's gotten pretty well acquainted with you. Well enough to tell the difference. If you got in that car, his first words would be, 'What are you doing here, Selena?'"

"No, they won't," she contradicted. "For Jeff, we're worlds apart. It would never occur to him that I could step into Gilly's shoes. The times I've been with him, even when we talked about Gilly, he's never been struck by the resemblance. You're an artist, conscious of bones, shapes, formation. Jeff doesn't look at women that way. He'll never see me through the make-up."

"It's better than a mask," Quinn corroborated. "That big red mouth, those smoky eyes. Even knowing that the other one's dead, I could almost be fooled. She looks like a real floozy." He winked at Selena. "In context, that's a compliment."

"Gilly has a coat with a fox collar." While they talked she had moved to the closet, was examining its contents. "High and fluffy. Turned up and buttoned at the throat, it will hide my face almost to the eyes."

"And the mascara already hides them," Quinn added.

"Besides, he'll never get a good look at me. It's dark out now. I don't suppose the side entrance to the drugstore is brightly lighted."

"No," Hugh conceded. "Only a dim bulb."

"And it will be dark inside his car." She handed the coat to Quinn, reached again into the closet. "Here's a hat with a floppy brim. I can pull it down on the left side, the side that will be nearest him, till it almost meets the coat collar."

"Like Garbo, she'll be," said Quinn. "Only the accent's different."

"Oh, I don't say I could deceive him if he were suspicious. But he'll have no reason to be. He believes he just talked to Gilly on the phone, made an appointment to meet her. When I step into his car, there'll be no question of my identity, he'll take me for granted. And he won't want to linger at the curb, where people can watch us. Once he starts the car his eyes will be on the road, the traffic. All I have to do is keep from saying anything that will give the show away. With my amnesia as an excuse for silence, that will be easy."

"It won't work," Hugh said. "I know it won't work."

"Maybe not," Selena answered. "I think it will, but in this business, nothing carries a guarantee. But the worst that can happen is that he'll know I'm not Gilly. Then I won't get any of the information we're after. We'll have moved neither forward nor back. You can still try to squeeze an explanation from him as to why he wanted to see Gilly in such a hurry. And if he recognizes me—well, all I'll have lost is my cover."

"And maybe you wouldn't consider that a loss," Hugh said acidly. "It would force you out into the open, wouldn't it? You'd have a chance to clear yourself of the charges he made last night. Could that have something to do with your pushing that plan? Could it be that you're anxious to try it—and fail?"

"You know that's unfair," she said. "As unfair as it would be for me to accuse you of wanting to prove him guilty of treason for personal reasons."

"Then I retract," he said. "But it doesn't matter. This whole discussion is academic. Maybe you could fool the congressman, maybe not. We'll never know which of us is right about that. I'd be demented if I let you go outside under any pretext. It would be difficult enough to protect you if we let Stone into your apartment. But once you got in his car—you'd have had it."

"Not necessarily," Quinn interposed. "You can encircle a car."

"I can put ten cars around it and a helicopter over it. They can keep him in constant sight. But they'll have no control over what goes on inside. What you're suggesting is a suicide mission."

"I don't agree," Quinn said. "If it comes to a crisis, all she has to do is stop talking Southern, tell him who she really is and that we know she's with him and have the car under close observation. He won't kill her then, not unless he's a double-dyed fool."

"Maybe it is only a joy ride." Hugh switched position. "A few hours ago, Selena, you were sure he was innocent. Maybe you were right. In that case, you'd be deserting your post at a time when we might be about to net the real spies."

"If you believed that," she retorted, "you'd be urging me to go. You think Jeff's guilty. His anxiety to get Gilly off alone shakes my conviction that he isn't. But there's only one way to find out—by hearing what he has to say. That's why I have to meet him."

"Because you want to solve the case?" Hugh challenged. "Or because you want to know the truth about Stone?"

"Both," she admitted. "But solving the case comes first. It has to, doesn't it? If he's a traitor, in his position he can do the country irreparable damage."

"If he's a traitor," Hugh said, "we'll wring it out of him without any more help from you."

"Will you? He's a member of Congress. You can't pull him in, ask him questions, put him through a third degree. Not unless you've incontrovertible proof that your charges are true. And I can get that proof tonight. Otherwise what will you do? Let him keep on till he's Vice-President, President even?"

"She's right," Quinn put in. "You heard the man on the phone. He won't come here. But his message may be worth hearing. And the only way to get it is for Mahomet to go to the mountain. We know this man; he's a shrewd cookie. We've nothing on him now, nothing we can make stick. And he's out of our reach. Tonight may be our one chance to nail him."

"You could be wrong," she said. "He may be clear of all this. By going with him, I may miss the man I'm supposed to be waiting for. But that's not what you're worried about, Hugh, is it? Never mind. You don't have to decide. I'm not asking for orders—or permission. When he gets to that drugstore, I'll be waiting for him."

"You will not. You stay in that apartment until I tell you to leave."

"I've had another thought," Quinn said. "I'll go with her to the corner. It would be natural for a brother, especially one from the South, to walk along. Before she gets in the car, she can introduce me to the congressman. I'll say, 'hush ma mouf, yo' don' mean Representative Jeffrey R. Stone, the one evahbody says is goin' to be our nex' Vice-President.' He'll know I heard the name loud and clear and won't forget it. He can't pull anything fancy when he's left a witness behind who saw her go off with him. And of course you'll set up enough drugstore cowboys to make sure he doesn't kidnap us both at gunpoint."

"You can stop thinking," Hugh told him. "What I need from you is brawn, not brain. Your job is to make sure Selena doesn't go out of the apartment."

"You're suggesting, maybe, physical force?"

"If necessary."

"Good heavens, Hugh, that's ridiculous. I've made up my mind to go and nobody can stop me."

"Quinn can."

Quinn looked at her, made a grimace of resignation.

"You're the boss," he said. "You tell me to hold her back, I'll hold her back. But we may be blowing the big one. You know that, don't you?"

There was a long silence before Hugh spoke again.

"All right." The voice from the speaker was almost toneless. "I'll put the loungers on the sidewalk, the cars on the street, the chopper in the air. Stone made the call from his office, he's now driving out Constitution Avenue. The traffic is light, he should reach the drugstore right on schedule. The rest is up to you."

There was little to do in the way of preparation. The coat she had chosen had deep pockets. She put Gilly's billfold into one, her own unusually equipped cosmetic case into the other. She was maneuvering the hat over the bandage when Hugh's voice came for the last time through the speaker.

"Stone's out of the Park, turning up Massachusetts Avenue. Ten minutes will get him to the drugstore." The pause was so long that she thought he had finished. Then he added a final two words. "Good luck."

"I'll be all right," she answered. "He won't hurt me." But her voice held no more certainty than her thoughts.

Quinn stepped into the hall first, took a searching look up and down before he let her follow him. He pressed the elevator button and they stood together, eyes on the overhead panel that, with numbered lights, marked its progress from the lobby to the eighth floor. The door opened automatically, they entered the empty car and Quinn pressed "1." The door shut. The car started down.

Selena felt a sinking in her stomach that was unjustified by the smooth, slow descent. She was already regretting her victory in the argument with Hugh. He was, as Quinn said, the boss. It was his place to give orders, hers to receive them. Why hadn't she accepted his dictum, stayed in the apartment, done as she was told? Never had she gone on an assignment with such unease. And it was not the danger from which she now recoiled. She dreaded the thought of riding with Stone, hearing what he had to say. If he was a traitor, she didn't have to be the one to find him out. And if he wasn't, if his intentions tonight had nothing to do with spying— She closed her eyes, feeling a little faint. She didn't know which would be worse, to sit beside him and hear him reveal his treason or to be there, as Gilly, while he talked confidentially to the dead girl.

The elevator trembled to a stop. She opened her eyes to see the numbered panel. They had passed the seventh floor, were stopping at the sixth. Quinn moved in front of her, almost hiding her with his bulk, as the door once more opened. A tall man, meticulously groomed, his air of distinction enhanced by a graying mustache, joined them. He was hatless, carried a topcoat over his left arm.

"The service doesn't get any faster," he said genially to Quinn as the door closed behind him. Then he saw Selena.

"Ah, Miss Gilly, how nice to have you home again. We were worried about our little neighbor."

"Thank you. I'm mighty glad to be back."

"You don't recognize me, do you?" He smiled kindly. "Now don't be troubled about it. You'll have your memory back in no time, I don't doubt it. I'm Colonel Morgan from 608."

"Oh yes, of course, Colonel, I'm sorry to be so slow. This is my brother Eugene who got leave to come and stay with me."

"Delighted to meet you, young man." He extended his right hand to give Quinn's a firm shake. At the same time his left hand moved under his coat. Selena saw the muzzle of a gun, a flash of fire, a noiseless explosion. Quinn's hand went to his chest, he gave a muffled grunt and crumpled at her feet. Selena looked down at him, stunned, unbelieving, then up at the colonel. The gun was fully exposed now, pointing at her, but his face was still genial.

"Don't scream," he said softly. "I don't want to shoot you too. But I will if you make a commotion."

"You—you killed him!"

"I aimed at the heart. And it would be hard to miss at this range." He reached behind him to push the button marked "B" for basement. "Now," he told her, "I think you should have a little rest till we get to a place where we can talk without interruption. Because we're going to have a great deal to say to each other."

He had shifted the gun to his right hand. Now he put the other in his pocket, pulled out a handkerchief and what looked like a plastic capsule. He crushed the capsule in the handkerchief, reached out to press it against her nose and mouth. She was conscious of a sickeningly sweet vapor, then had a sensation of falling, falling. She clawed at the handkerchief, gasping for air. Above her the colonel's face ballooned to massive proportions. Darkness closed in and she was conscious of nothing at all.

CHAPTER TEN

Monday Night

The next thing she knew was a sharp ammonia odor in her nostrils, the sting of light slaps on her cheeks. She opened her eyes to see the colonel's face close to hers.

"Ah," he said approvingly, "she's with us again." The words were spoken over her shoulder to a man she couldn't see who was holding her crossed arms behind her back, supporting her limp form against him. "That's right, breathe deep." The colonel continued to wave a small vial under her nose. "It will clear your head. Then we can have our little chat."

"Where—where am I?"

"The classic question." But he didn't answer it. "Let's see if she can stand alone." The other man, still pinioning her arms, stepped away. "That's right, lean her against the window ledge. That should give her enough support. But don't let her go over. Not yet."

Cold stone rubbed against her back, cold air struck her shoulders. They were in a three-sided alcove of gray stone. At her left a stairway spiraled downward. But her sense of being in an ancient tower prison was canceled by the spacious elevator, its door wide open, into which she faced. She had not yet seen or heard the man beside her but had felt with a sinking certainty that the hands holding her wrists in a tight, hurting grip must be those of Jeff Stone. Now he spoke for the first time and relief that the voice was strange softened the impact of his words.

"Five hundred and fifty-five feet to the ground," he said. "And this time it's all solid pavement, with no tree to break your fall."

She twisted round to look beyond him. He had removed the metal-framed glass to leave a hole more than large enough to justify the colonel's warning. Through it she looked out on a panorama of Washington, on one side the new Smithsonian Museum, on the other a wide expanse of parks split by the steady stream of cars on Constitution Avenue. And on the ground far, far below, giant searchlights pointed upward to outline in white radiance the shaft in which they stood.

"We're at the top of the Washington Monument," she said in surprise.

"Right on the first guess," the colonel agreed. "Most popular view in the city and you're getting a special preview. The regular tourists won't get up here after dark until it goes on summer hours."

"She'll get a special preview, too," the other man said with unpleasant humor, "of the way it looks on the outside, top to bottom."

"Suicides repeat themselves," the colonel told her. "Pill takers go on taking pills. Shooters get another gun. The psychologists will nod their heads when they hear that as soon as you got out of the hospital, you started looking for a new jumping-off place. You can turn her loose, Breck. The only way she can go now is down."

"How did I get here?" She rubbed her freed hands together to restore circulation, then pressed her fingers against her forehead as if to ease an aching head. Her left thumb touched the bandage-covered button that started the tiny tape recorder rolling. If only, she thought despairingly, it were a radio instead, carrying what they said at once to Hugh's ears. But at least if they did throw her over, their words would go with her, be found when she was.

"Easy," the colonel answered. "After you passed out in the elevator, I took you to the basement garage. Breck was waiting there with the car and we brought you here under a robe."

"But how did you get in? Isn't the Monument locked at night?"

"Of course, but I've an excellent sense of timing. There's a guard on duty who checks in by phone to the central office at ten minutes before every hour. Then he goes out to the grounds to take a look around. He had the misfortune to meet Breck there and now he's having a little nap on a bench on the ground floor. We have his key, which opens all locks. Tomorrow he'll have a story about being mugged and robbed. Together with your suicide that will make the Monument a greater tourist attraction than ever."

"You brought me here to kill me?"

"I brought you here for two reasons. Because it fits your already established suicide pattern. And because it's an ideal place to talk, isolated, inaccessible, a place where no one would think to look for you—assuming, that is, you're missed."

"My—my brother—what's become of him?"

"We dumped the body in a storage closet in the basement. It may be days before he's found."

"Oh." She swallowed hard, tried to shake off the vision of Quinn's body dropping at her feet, forced herself to go on. "When he's—when they find him, they'll know he was murdered. It will seem funny to have that happen and me—kill myself the same night."

"Lots of things will seem funny," he admitted. "But I don't mind leaving them with questions, as long as they don't have answers. And that's what we're here to discuss. What answers did you give them, Gilly?"

"Answers? I don't know what you're talking about."

"I think you do. I think you know more than you pretend. We can stay here for an hour. It'll be longer than that before

164

the man at the other end begins to wonder why the guard hasn't made his next check-in call. I think you'll be able to remember quite a bit in that time."

"I'm trying to remember," she said. "I've been trying ever since yesterday."

"That blank look you gave me when I got on the elevator seemed genuine. I don't think you had any idea who I was. Do you now?"

"I—I'm sure I've seen you before." Again she pressed her hand to her forehead, put on an expression of seeking. "You're familiar somehow. But I don't believe you're a neighbor. You're not Colonel Morgan. You don't live in 608."

"Correct, in triplicate. My friends do call me colonel, though. It's an honorary title. Self-bestowed. Does the name Jonathan Klee ring a bell?"

It rang an entire belfry. What the name meant to Gilly she didn't know, but to Selena he was a man she'd never met but had heard of often. A shadowy figure on the fringes of government. Lobbyist for a variety of interests and industries. What a perfect cover, she thought with unwilling admiration, for espionage! An influence peddler whose job is contacts, who works constantly with insiders in Congress, the Defense Department, all the branches of government. He can show an open interest—because they may affect his clients—in defense contracts, bases, treaties. Buying and selling is his way of life. He can, without betraying his foreign alliance, probe the soft spots, find men in the legislative and executive offices who will, for a fee, reveal secrets to help his business clients. And among them he can seek those who might, for a larger sum, betray their country.

"Ah!" He noted the flash of recognition she could not hide. "A light dawns. You know me now."

"I—I think so." She blinked as if finding it hard to focus. "I think I've done some work for you." She took a chance on one of the associations the name had for her. "Was it—something to do with oil?"

"Oil?" He frowned, then brightened. "Oh yes! You did a good job for us on those leases. That was a long time ago. Your memory for the past is better than my own."

"It's spotty," she said. "Things come and go."

"That's what I'm interested in," he said. "Not past history but what's come and gone about the days before your—fall."

"How about that, Colonel?" Breck interrupted to indicate a helicopter floating to the north of them. "You think it could be a search party?"

"It could be," the colonel said carelessly. "But it's probably the White House ferry. It doesn't matter which. We're under cover here. They can fly all around us and not see a thing."

Selena put her hands in her pockets, found them empty. She ran her tongue around dry lips.

"I've lost my make-up kit," she said pathetically. "I'm sure I brought it with me. And I just know I've bitten off all my lipstick."

"How about that for a dame!" Breck exclaimed. "A quarter of an hour away from hell and she's worried about her looks."

"This type of dame," the colonel told him, "will worry about her looks even in hell." He turned back to her. "I'm glad that you brought it up. It would be right in character for you to put on fresh make-up before jumping. Your kind wants to look seductive even smattered all over the concrete. So give her back the kit, Breck. It will be another checkpoint for the psychologists. We went through your pockets to make sure you weren't carrying a gun or anything else that would interfere with us. But it's better for you to be found with all the things you'd naturally be carrying. Give her the wallet too. It will make identification easier and I like to be helpful to the police whenever I can."

She took the objects Breck held out, put the wallet in her pocket and unzipped the kit. She took out mirror and lipstick and, with unsteady fingers, thickly coated her lips with red. Then she put both into the case and, without drawing the zipper, returned it to her pocket.

"Now you're set for another beauty contest," the colonel said. "So we can get back to business. I want to hear all that you've remembered and told. And to whom."

"I haven't told anybody. Just now—talking to you—things are beginning to come back to me."

"Maybe you're telling the truth," he said. "It's possible you woke up with your mind a blank so far as our dealings are concerned. I got a psychiatrist's opinion on that. He said it's not unusual for a person to block out all persons, places and things connected with something disagreeable. But then again, maybe you're lying."

While he spoke her hand came out of her pocket, lipstick hidden in tight clenched fist. She put the hand behind her back, as if to serve as a cushion against the stone. The lipstick, flashbulb at the top, pointed diagonally over the ledge and toward the sky. It was shielded by her body from visibility to the men inside. She pressed the button, held it, let it go, pressed and held again, pressed and did not hold, then pressed and held. She let it stay dark for half a minute, then repeated the cycle and went through it again and again throughout their conversation.

"Why would I lie?"

"That's what we're about to find out. It occurs to me that you may have awakened remembering everything you knew when you went to sleep. And that you told your story to the police or the FBI or some other agency who concocted the amnesia story and sent you home to await developments. It was the possibility that they might be waiting with you that made us reluctant to visit you in your apartment. We preferred to have you come to us."

"Is that why Jeff—why Congressman Stone phoned—in order to get me away from my apartment?"

"The congressman was of great assistance. We're deeply in his debt."

"I'm sure you are." Whatever she'd been hoping, the hope died. "You're spies, aren't you, all of you? Spies and traitors."

"We're businessmen," he corrected. "If you hadn't had that unfortunate streak of patriotism, we could still be doing business together."

"Was it you," she asked, "who pushed me off the bridge?"

"So you remember being pushed."

"I remember—I was on the bridge. There was somebody— we were fighting." She looked at him, shook her head. "Now it's gone again. Was it you?"

"No, I've never laid a finger on you. Until today."

Her glance moved to the squat, ugly man who now stood near the elevator. "Was it—"

"No, this is your first meeting with Breck."

"Then it must have been—" She had to force herself to complete the question. "Was it Congressman Stone?"

His head went back in a laugh that showed sincere amusement.

"I think she really doesn't remember," he told Breck. "Either that or she's a better actress than anyone ever gave her credit for." He turned back to Selena. "If you're feeding me a line, you're not as stupid as I thought you. Maybe that crack on the head knocked in a few brains."

"I never was stupid." A show of indignation seemed in order. "Just because a girl has looks doesn't mean she has to be dumb. I was always smart enough to take care of myself."

"You were," he conceded, "until last week you got a little too smart."

"What happened?" she begged. "I wish you'd tell me. Who threw me off the bridge? Why did he do it? And why do you want to kill me now?"

"You said it yourself. You called us spies and traitors."

"Yes, I did." She squeezed her eyes shut, opened them.

"For a minute it seemed as if you were. But now it's gone again. You're just a man who hired me to—to be nice to people and find out things."

"A pity," he said, "you couldn't go on thinking that. You were a good worker. I'm sorry to lose you."

"Then why—"

"It may be gone now. I'm inclined to think it is. You're not sharp enough to run a bluff this long. Or smart enough to figure out anything for yourself. If Travers had kept his mouth shut, you'd still think it was a routine assignment."

"Travers?"

"Yes, Travers." He was impatient. "Now don't say that name doesn't mean anything to you?"

"I know Mr. Travers, of course," she said with dignity. "He works for Mr. Stone."

"That's right," he said bluntly. "And he threw you off Calvert Bridge."

"Mr. Travers did?"

"You were there, I wasn't. But he claims the credit."

"I don't understand. Why would Mr. Travers want to kill me?"

"Still blacked out, eh? I thought the name might start a train of recollections."

She turned to look out over the ledge. The helicopter had disappeared. Her finger had grown numb on the flashlight button, but she continued its blinking.

"Now listen to me, Gilly," Klee said. "I can't waste any more time. You've nothing to gain by lying. Whom have you told about our little deal?"

"I haven't told anybody. How could I when I don't even remember what the deal was?"

"Travers said that when he let it slip that you were acting as go-between to get information for the communists instead of for a business firm, you got hysterical, said you were going to report it, get us all in trouble. That's why he had to try to kill you. Too bad he botched the job."

"I don't remember any of that. I guess it's the way you say the psychiatrist said. It's just too terrible to remember."

"More terrible things than that can happen," he said softly. "I know from the way you acted with Travers that you're a noble young woman willing to sacrifice yourself for your country. So you'd do your best to cooperate with the agents, go along with the amnesia act and pretend that you've given away none of my secrets. But it's essential for me to have the facts. Because if what you say is true, if you've told nobody anything, then your death will end it. I can go along with business as usual. But if you've given me away, I'll have to start packing. You can see how important it is for me to have an accurate picture. I don't want to run from a shadow. Unless there's a noose behind it."

"How could I tell anybody what I don't remember?"

"Now your question," he continued reasonably, "is why should you help me? If you're going to die anyway, you might as well upset my applecart. That's why I brought Breck along. He's a specialist in answering that kind of question."

"That's right," Breck seconded. "None better. You notice something, Colonel? One of those searchlights is acting crazy. Like it's about to go out."

"Then they'll send an electrician. But we'll be gone long before he gets here."

Selena too had noticed the searchlight. It flickered on and off as if about to fail. Only an insider would notice that the flickering had sequence. The same sequence that she, with her flashlight, had been producing. She let her own light go out, slid it back into her coat.

"I'm giving you one more. chance," Klee said, "to answer voluntarily. Whom did you talk to about me and what did you tell them?"

"Nothing," she said. "Cross my heart." Completion of the childish oath hung unspoken between them.

"How long do you need, Breck?"

"Five minutes. Maybe less."

"I'm sorry, Gilly." The colonel sounded as if he meant it. "I'd like to avoid this unpleasantness. But I have to know my position with absolute certainty. If, after five minutes of Breck's specialty, you still say that you don't remember and haven't told, I'll be satisfied it's the truth. Now, have you anything to say before he goes to work?"

She looked at Breck, who stood flexing his fingers, his face impassive, waiting for orders. Help, the searchlight had told her, was on its way. But how soon? Five minutes from now? Or later? Would Breck's expertise, in that time, force her to drop the mask, admit her real identity? It was a revelation that, made to Stone, should have saved her life. With these two men it would have an opposite effect. Klee had said too much to let her live, no matter what her name. And once he knew she was not the injured Gilly, her bandage would become suspect. They would remove it, search it for contraband. She would go to her death minus the taped record without which the capture of Klee and Breck might prove only half a victory. She needed to hold them off, to gain time.

And one other thing was necessary. The Monument's one elevator stood, door open, in front of her. The only way to reach her was by the stairs. And anyone coming up would be clearly visible, an unmissable target for two armed and desperate men. There was, in fact, no way to rescue her. The sensible plan would be to stay at the bottom. Sooner or later the quarry would have to come down, walk into their waiting guns. And then, she thought, the only one lost will be me. Yet she could not believe that, with Hugh in charge, the chosen plan would be to wait. It was up to her to provide a third choice.

"Well, my dear," Klee said. "It appears you have nothing to tell me. So—" He nodded to Breck.

"No!" She pulled from her coat pocket Gilly's billfold and, in a sudden movement, turned to fling it through the window.

"What the hell!" Klee moved to catch her arm but was too late. Together they watched the red leather plummet downward.

"What was that?" he demanded angrily.

"My money case."

"And what do you think you'll gain by throwing it out?"

"I wrote a message on a dollar bill," she lied. "With the point of my lipstick. It says 'Klee killed me.' When they find my body, they'll find that too. Then they'll know."

"You should have watched her closer," Breck chided. "I noticed she was fidgeting something terrible, with her hands in back of her."

"Thank you for telling me," Klee snapped, "now that it's too late."

"I figured she had plenty of reason to fidget," Breck returned. "How would I know she was writing something?"

"I very much doubt," Klee said, "that a message written under such adverse circumstances will be legible. It's probably just a smear."

"Maybe so," she conceded. "But it's a chance."

"Yes, it's a chance I can't take. Breck, go down and get the wallet."

"Me, Colonel? I've a job to do here."

"It'll keep. Her fall may be seen, draw a crowd. We'll have to clear out in a hurry, we can't stop to search the ground around her. And we can't leave it as possible evidence against me. So you'll have to pick it up now, before she goes over. Get moving."

Breck stepped into the elevator, closed the door. Klee waited till he started down, then turned back to Selena.

"That was stupid of both of us," he said. "Me to let you get away with it. And you to think it would do you any good. In a way, though, it's rather reassuring. I don't think you'd have gone to so much trouble to put my name on record if you'd already talked about me to the authorities. It firms up my confidence in your amnesia."

"In that case," she said, "maybe you'll tell me some of the things I've forgotten. You say you have to kill me because I called you spies and traitors. And I think you must be. But I don't know why I think so. Or how I was involved. Or what Mr. Travers had to do with it. Or Congressman Stone."

"You really have no memory of last Tuesday night? You don't remember being with Travers? Or trying to get to Stone?"

At each question she shook her head, moving imperceptibly to her left so that, in order to face her, he stood with his back to the elevator.

"You called me a go-between," she said. "And that sounds right. I was always being a go-between."

"Indeed you were. And an excellent one."

"But not for spying. I never did that. Did I?"

"Not knowingly. And not at all until recently. We needed someone to carry papers from Travers to us and cash from us to Travers."

"But why bring me into it? You can go to the Capitol whenever you like. You have business there. Nobody would think anything wrong if they saw you with Mr. Travers."

"Travers would. In this business when you hire a new man, it's smart to stay nameless and faceless until you're sure you can trust him. I wasn't going to put Travers into a blackmailer's seat by letting him know who was buying until he was too deeply enmeshed to pull out with a whole skin. So I sent you up with word that you knew someone who was willing to pay a high price for any data he could wring from the Joint Committee hearings. For you it was no different from any other job. You didn't know what the hearings were about. But Travers did. He knew there was no customer for that information on this side of the Pacific. And he made the mistake of letting you know."

173

"Why did he tell me?"

"That's a question you could answer better than I, if you could remember. I have only his version of what happened last Tuesday and I think it's been expurgated. He says he thought you knew what you were doing, that he dropped the word 'spies' carelessly, not dreaming he was giving anything away. Maybe that's the way it was. Maybe not. My guess is that he wasn't concerned about what you knew or didn't know. He was sending a message to me that he was fully aware of what we were doing and was about to press for higher pay. Does that bring anything back?"

"No."

"I wish it did. I'd like a true report on your conversation with Travers. It would clue me on how to deal with him. In fact, I'll bargain with you. If you can pull out of your subconscious exactly what Travers said, I'll cancel your upcoming session with Breck. Believe me, that's an offer worth taking."

"I can't," she said. "I can't remember talking to Mr. Travers at all. And I don't know what—what Congressman Stone had to do with it. Was he—"

The sound of the arriving elevator stopped her.

"Breck made good time," Klee said. He turned without haste as the door slid open. "I'm curious to see this lipstick writing, whether we can read—"

Selena held her breath. Was it Breck returning—or someone else? For an instant Klee's body blocked her view. But his quick tensing, the lightning movement of his hand toward his gun gave her the answer. He didn't make it. Another gun flashed and his arm went limp at his side. He turned enough so that she could see past him into the elevator, see Hugh, his face hard, his gun trained on the colonel. She was suddenly dizzy, numb, without strength. The face of Hugh blurred, her knees gave way and, for the second time that night, she sank unconscious to the floor.

CHAPTER ELEVEN

Tuesday

"It was," Hugh told her, "somewhat of a fox-goose-bag of grain problem." He was sitting in Selena's den sipping coffee while he filled in the gaps of the past night's events. "Should I leave you passed out on the floor while I took Klee into custody? Or let him stay at large while I carried you away?"

"A real dilemma. How did you resolve it?"

"I had no choice," he said without regret. "I was forced to shoot him in the knee to make sure he'd stay put until I could send someone for him. I might have been more careful not to shatter the bone if I'd known he hadn't actually hurt you, that your fainting spell was from relief."

"I was terribly frightened."

"Out of everything but your wits evidently. They were functioning at full speed. It was particularly thoughtful of you to send the elevator down for me. I used to climb those 898 steps as a Boy Scout, but I'm past the age when it would be a fun thing. Also it was useful to have Mr. Breck in hand before I started up to tell me what I'd find at the top. Your best work, though, was with the flashlight. Until your signal started flashing we had no idea where you were." His eyes met hers and the note of flippancy dropped from his voice. "My God, Selena, you can't imagine what it was like, knowing you were gone! And it was my fault. I had a man in the garage, but after you got the phone call I moved him. I was totally focused on the congressman, had my entire staff deployed along the route to your rendezvous or ready to trail his car in any direction. Then I got word that you weren't on the way to the drugstore and we hadn't a clue as to where to start looking."

"Was it long before you missed me?"

"Too long. I had two men waiting at the bus stop in front of the apartment building. Their job was to cover you against attack from a passing car when you stepped out of doors. I alerted them to your leaving Gilly's apartment, but they couldn't pinpoint the time it would take for you to get an elevator and ride down. The lobby's small, has only one entrance and we'd made sure it was empty. With Quinn as your escort, I didn't anticipate any danger between the eighth floor and the sidewalk. Well, that's the human error I said could happen. Only I didn't expect it to be my own."

"Then it was the men on the street who let you know I hadn't come out?"

"Yes. Two minutes too late. We dragnetted the building, found no traces, knew you must have gone by car through the garage exit. There was nothing to indicate the kind of car, who was in it or where he was taking you. At first I thought Quinn was still with you, had some hope that he'd be able to manage an escape."

"And then you—you found him."

"Yes." His face darkened. "He was one of my best men."

"That was my fault. You didn't want me to go. If I hadn't insisted, overridden your objections—"

"Quinn was as determined to go as you," Hugh cut her short. "I wouldn't have given in to your arguments. But when he backed you up, I was pushed into a corner. No, Selena, don't blame yourself. Quinn was doing a job, one he chose with full knowledge of the risks. And I think he'd say we had fair exchange for his life. Lacking what you and Quinn did, Klee would still be free and not one but thousands of lives might be forfeit. We caught him just in time."

"Before the information from the Joint Committee got out of the country?"

"The attack on Gilly froze their operation. As long as she was alive and they didn't know what she had told or was about to tell, Klee had to live with the possibility that he was hot. He couldn't contact his next in line or pass anything on. Word of her death would have set him free. He was poised for action as soon as the announcement came through. If you hadn't stepped into her shoes on Sunday, the Red Chinese would be able to outguess us on a long front."

"The colonel told you this? You were able to make him talk?"

"We let him hear a playback of the tape from your bandage. With so much on record, he had nothing to gain from reticence. We also found Travers very talkative. Breck didn't know much, but he added a few details. Between them we've been able to piece together a fairly clear picture. Klee's been lobbying most of his life. He made the leap to espionage about a year ago and was able to use many of the old techniques, some of the old sources. And it was much more lucrative. Until this month he'd had no dealings with Travers. He'd been able to get what he wanted from old established stands."

"Do you know who they are too?"

"Oh yes. He was generous with other men's names. The boys are fanning out over town now, rounding them up. We won't break the news of what happened last night until we have them all in custody. There aren't many and most of them are in small jobs, but from time to time information of value crosses their desks. In each case Klee found a weakness he could play on."

"Is that how it was with Mr. Travers?"

"Klee carried one of the main rules of lobbying over into his new game. Develop a source before you need it; you never know who'll prove useful. Travers was a poker player.

They invited him to Harmony Hall and let him win a few hundred. Then he began losing. Thousands. So he was ripe for an approach long before Klee made it."

"And then he didn't go himself. He sent Gilly."

"That's right. He'd used her a number of times, on lobbying jobs, found her willing and not too bright. Also she was well known in Stone's office. So it was natural to turn to her when he wanted something from Travers. She was a good messenger who never asked questions about what he wanted or how he was going to use it. First, about a week before the hearings opened, he sent her to ask for a position paper Stone had received from State."

"The one you said your plant in the opposition camp had already seen."

"Actually, it was fairly unimportant and we haven't been harmed by its slipping through. The colonel was using it as a test case to find out whether he could count on Travers when he really needed him. If the man had balked then, that would have ended it. But he was deep in debt and his creditors were pressing him—Klee saw to that—so he handed it over and took his pay. Then they set up the same arrangement—Travers to Gilly to Klee—for everything he could get from the Joint Committee."

"What went wrong?"

"The usual thing. Greed. Nothing was said about espionage, but of course Travers knew the score. On Monday he gave her several papers, including a map, the one you discovered had been copied at Harmony Hall. On Tuesday night he had to work late, but when he finally got away from the office he drove by her apartment and picked her up. She brought him payment, in cash, for Monday's delivery and he turned over the new data in an envelope with Stone's name on it. Trouble is, he then counted the money and decided it wasn't enough. He told her to inform her principal that if the price wasn't doubled, there'd be no more deliveries. She started to argue, said it was the largest amount of cash she'd ever carried, that it seemed a very liberal payment for such a little bit of information. And that's when the rocket went up. Travers said it wasn't the amount of information but the risk he was taking that had to determine the pay scale. Treason carried a heavy penalty. Gilly was horrified. She couldn't believe she was involved with spying. Unluckily for her, he convinced her that nobody but the communists would buy what he was selling. That sent her near to hysterics. She said she was going to take the paper he'd just given her, go to Stone and tell him the whole thing. He pulled over to the curb, stopped the car, grabbed her purse and took the envelope out. She snatched it away from him, got out of the car and ran. They were about two blocks southeast of Calvert Bridge at the time. He followed her on foot, caught up with her as she reached the bridge. What the police saw as they drove up from the other side was the two of them fighting for the envelope. Travers got it, all but the scrap that was torn off and found in her hand. Then he saw the police car coming and knew she had to be silenced. He lifted her up, pushed her over the rail and got out of there. He was in a blue funk by then. As soon as he got back to his own apartment he put both the cash and the envelope down the incinerator. So he never knew the envelope was torn."

"But if Gilly was his only link with the spy ring, if he didn't even know the colonel's name, how could he notify them about what had happened?"

"He couldn't. Klee learned of Gilly's injury the same way everyone else did. From the newscast the next morning. He knew she'd been due to meet Travers, to pay him off and get more information, so he was able to jump to a reasonably accurate conclusion as to what had happened. He made a luncheon date with Travers, ostensibly to discuss tax relief for one of his corporations, suggested they drive out to the country. In the car he accused him of throwing Gilly off the bridge and Travers gave him a watered-down version of the facts. He also told him what Klee was most anxious to know—that Gilly had gone over empty-handed and he'd burned the cash and data. So they felt sure the suicide story would stick, since there was no evidence pointing in any other direction."

"Wasn't the colonel taking a chance in letting Travers know who he was? That's exactly what he'd been trying to avoid by using Gilly as middleman."

"What he'd been trying to avoid," Hugh answered, "was putting himself in Travers' power. The attack on Gilly made Travers the outlaw, stopped him from betraying anyone else. Gilly was the big threat to them both. If she died without talking, they could feel secure. But when there began to be reports of her improvement, their nerves were stretched taut. There was nothing Travers could do to stop her from talking; he had to leave everything in Klee's hands. It was, of course, one of Klee's lieutenants who sent the gunman to the hospital Friday night. When that failed and when they heard she was conscious again, Klee knew he would have to handle it himself. Either that or get out of the country. And he couldn't bring himself to abandon his highly successful operation while there was still a chance of salvaging it. You know the rest of the story better than I do. You lived through it."

"Not all of it." She felt oddly constrained from bringing up Jeff's name, had hoped an explanation of his role would be included in Hugh's report. Now he was finished and she was forced to ask the question. "I still don't understand Congressman Stone's part in the conspiracy."

"Ah yes, Stone." His measuring glance made her sure that the omission had not sprung from forgetfulness. "That was the last question on your tape recorder before I popped out of the elevator. I hate to have to tell you this—" He paused and she knew with self-annoyance that she was visibly holding her breath. "He's clean. The only thing he's guilty of is bad judgment."

"That's not possible. He must have been working with them."

"Believe me, if he had been, I'd know it." Hugh spoke with feeling. "I wasn't exactly in this as his defense counsel. But if Klee'd had Stone on his string, he wouldn't have bothered with Travers. A secretary's access to information is relatively limited. In addition to which, Travers is an unstable character. It was his panicking on Tuesday night that landed them in this jam."

"That may be good Harvard logic," she returned. "But it doesn't make sense. It was Jeff who phoned Gilly and—or was I mistaken about that? Was it someone else mimicking his voice? But it couldn't have been. Your men saw him leave his office, drive to the drugstore."

"That's right. It was Stone who called."

"Well, then— Oh, stop being a comedian! You know I'm anxious to know his role. Don't make it so hard for me."

"I'm not trying to make it hard. I'm just reluctant to restore him to membership in the Hound's Tooth Club. And he comes out of this case without a stain on his character."

"How can that be? It was his phone call that got me out of the apartment and into Klee's hands. If he wasn't part of their team, why would he set Gilly up for them like that?"

"He didn't know he was setting up anybody. It was just one of those breaks that come along. A good break, Klee thought. A bad one, as it turned out. The only thing that motivated the congressman's call was the fact that he wanted to see her."

"Why?"

"He broke out in a rash of conscience. For him a rare and overdue malady, I'd say. He'd been brooding over what he thought was Gilly's attempt at suicide and apparently what you said about her possible pregnancy struck a nerve. He was worried about being responsible for the girl's death wish. So as soon as he learned she was out of the hospital, he decided to find out whether she really had jumped on his account and, more important, whether she intended to try again. If so, he intended to offer to marry her when and if his divorce came through."

"That was very decent of him."

"Very," he said dryly. "That's an advantage heels have. One decent act turns one into a hero. Unhappily for heroes, it's also vice versa."

"If that's why he called, if he wasn't cooperating with the colonel, why did he insist on Gilly's coming out to meet him?"

"The reason he gave on the phone was the true one. His self-abnegation hadn't reached the point of willingness to run a gauntlet of any reporters or cameramen who might be lurking about. Later, if he married her, he'd have to face a bad press. But by then her news value would have been reduced. He wasn't going to start the headlines any earlier than he had to. And of course if she'd told him that he wasn't to blame for her leap, he'd have been out of it entirely."

"Did he tell you all that himself?"

"Not me. We missed a direct confrontation by inches. He drove up to the drugstore almost simultaneously with our discovery that you'd vanished. So I had him pulled out of his car and taken to our nearest back room. We thought then he was our one key to locating you. So as soon as we finished searching the building I set out to join him. I was going to take personal charge of his interrogation, without benefit of congressional immunity. But before I got there the helicopter sent down word that someone was flashing the dash-dash-dot-dash code from the top of the Washington Monument. It had to be you. So I forgot the congressman and headed for the Monument. We put a chain of cars on all the roads around it and two of us went in."

"It was you," she said, "who blinked the Q signal with one of the searchlights."

"Yes. I didn't know what I'd find at the top, how many were with you or what they were doing. But I figured if you had advance notice, you could at least move out of the line of fire. Of course, you did much better than that. By sending down Breck, you gave me both transportation and a *modus operandi*. Incidentally, we picked up Gilly's wallet, but there was no lipstick on any of the bills."

"Naturally not. I was much too busy with the flashlight to write any notes. Making the colonel think I'd written one was all that was needed."

"Indeed it was. It was a brilliant gesture."

"I'm ashamed that I behaved so stupidly when you got there. Seeing you, knowing it was ended, suddenly it was all too much."

"You held up just long enough," he said. "You were entitled to a spell of weakness."

"What puzzles me, though, is how the colonel was able to take advantage of Jeff's phone call. Had he been waiting in the hall all the time, on the chance that Gilly would go out?"

"No, he'd been in his own hotel—a mile away—trying to work out a plan of action. Travers was the catalyst. He listened in on his extension when Stone put the call through to Gilly. As soon as the congressman was on his way, Travers ducked out to a pay phone and notified the colonel. He and Breck left at once for Gilly's building, drove into the garage right after my man transferred from there to the street. Then all he had to do was ride up to the sixth floor, wait beside the elevator till the indicator showed a stop at eight, push the button and get on. That's what he meant when he said they were in Stone's debt. His call gave you to them by special delivery."

"But since it ended in their capture, in closing the case, we're really the ones who are indebted to him."

"That's strictly feminine logic," Hugh returned. "Stone gave us, purely by accident, a bit of assistance and he's innocent of treason. But that doesn't make him a great man. Maybe you should hear his explanation of why he was willing to marry Gilly. Here's the direct quote: 'Since all women are whores, I might as well marry a card-carrying one. At least, there'll be no surprises.'"

"Oh." She felt a sudden chill. "He was thinking of me."

"I thought that might put him in new perspective."

"Put him—" She stared at him, astonished. "You expected me to feel insulted, to turn against him? But it's my fault. This is something I've done to him. I was his last resort and I—I failed him."

"So we'll take up a collection and send him flowers."

"Please, Hugh, it's no joke. You say he was brooding about Gilly, about being responsible for her suicide. Well, I'm responsible for him. You can destroy a man by taking away his faith in everyone as surely as by driving him to jump off a bridge."

"He's a tough character. He'll survive."

"I've got to tell him, let him know how it really is, that I'm working for Section Q."

"Are you in love with the man, Selena? Do you want to marry him? Is that the problem?"

"No, it's not that. Can't you understand? I have a conscience too."

"I'm sure you have. But this is a case where there's only a choice of evils. You can break your own cover whenever you like, get out of Q and back to a peaceful existence. But that would do no good here. In order to explain our midnight meetings, you'd have to give me away too. And I can't let you do that."

"Why not? While he was suspected of being a traitor, it was out of the question, of course. But now he's been cleared.

You admit there's nothing against him, so why can't he be told?"

"Because he has no need to know."

"I realize you don't like him, but—"

"This has nothing to do with my not liking him. Nor with my being jealous of him, though that's a fact too. It's a basic, unbreakable rule. The man across the alley—though he may be a cad—is a loyal patriotic American. So are our other neighbors, our friends. But I work very hard to keep any of them from finding out who I am. You haven't even told your family about Q. That's the way it has to be. You know it as well as I do. If your happiness were at stake, your permanent happiness, I'd try to figure some way to clear you. But to salve the congressman's tender feelings, to restore his faith in women, no, Selena, that's not worth putting my job in jeopardy."

"I suppose you're right," she said slowly. "I guess there's nothing either of us can do."

"I've already done Stone one big favor. That's enough."

"What have you done for him?"

"One of my men went to Travers' apartment early this morning. He told him Gilly was dead, accused him of her murder, said we had proof of his treason. He got a full confession. Then he let him go alone into his bedroom to pack for jail. It's nine stories up, over a stone court. Travers went out the window, died instantly."

"Oh no!"

"It'll be in the afternoon papers. Suicide attributed to despondency over debts. No one saw my man go in, no one saw him come out. There'll be nothing to link Travers with Gilly, except the well-known fact that when a suicide leap gets headlines it puts ideas in other people's heads."

"Did you want him to jump?"

"We gave him the opportunity and he took it. I wasn't deliberately trying to protect the congressman, but that's one of the effects of Travers' death. Having his secretary involved in espionage would have shattered his image. More than that, it would have brought the security issue into this summer's campaign and, as I said before, Q has to stay outside politics. Also it would be difficult to try him for Gilly's murder since we're sticking with the story that she died in the Washington Monument."

"Poor Gilly. She'll be able to have a funeral now."

"With a twenty-one-gun salute. When we release the story of breaking up the spy ring, it will star her as heroine."

"I'm glad. What story are you telling?"

"As close to the truth as we can stay. We've made no alterations in the story that's already been published, from the time of her being found under the bridge to her going home yesterday. She remembered nothing, hadn't told anyone anything, but she had a premonition, a sense of fear, without knowing what she was afraid of. So she arranged to have a private detective go home with her and pose as her brother. That's a checkable fact, since Quinn did have a private license. It was one of his best covers. There's no end of places you can get into when you're tracing errant husbands. We won't have to mention the congressman's call. All we say is that Gilly and Quinn left her apartment and got into the elevator. Where they were going is anybody's guess. Klee intercepted them, shot Quinn and abducted Gilly. Clever deduction on the part of security agents, about which we'll go into no detail, tracked them to the top of the Monument. When the agent got there he found her on the floor and carried her down. The doctor pronounced her dead on arrival. Since there's not going to be a trial for her murder we don't have to be precise about the cause of death. But we'll make it definite that Klee had employed her in his lobbying activities, that it was her discovery of and protest against his involvement in espionage that led to her being pushed off the bridge. We may have to be vague about the details, but we'll leave no doubt that she died for her country. Because she did."

"I don't see how you can keep Travers' name out of it when Klee knows about him. Won't he talk?"

"Not unless he thinks it will help his own case. And from where he sits it would appear to have the opposite effect. The last he saw of the girl he thinks was Gilly she was being scooped up from the Monument floor. Talking about Travers' throwing her from the bridge isn't going to change the fact that she apparently recovered from that, was O.K. when Klee picked her up, and died in his custody. We're charging him with Quinn's murder and the evidence on that is clear. The bullet matches the gun in his pocket. A man can only hang once, but even so he's not likely to want to add Gilly's death to the indictment against him. So I don't expect Klee to try to amend the official version. And when security is involved, the press doesn't expect answers to every question. Some areas can stay in shadow."

"One thing you've overlooked," she said. "Klee saw you, plain and undisguised, as a security agent."

"And if Klee can, why not Stone? Is that the argument?"

"I'm not arguing. It just now occurred to me. I thought maybe you hadn't realized it."

"Oh yes, it came to me right afterward that I'd broken the basic unbreakable rule. While you were a missing person, I forgot all the rules. Fortunately, it cost nothing. Klee never saw me before, never will again. The glimpse he got of me lasted thirty seconds in a dim light. Then I got you out of there and Klee had bullets in his arm and his leg to occupy his mind. The man I sent up was an open agent, one who can testify in court. Klee has no idea there was a switch. He thinks the same man who went down with you came up for him. But your point is well taken—if it is a point. If I'm going to be that careless with my identity—and it was careless; someone else could have rescued you as well as I—then I ought to let you unburden your conscience by passing it on to Stone. How important is it to you, Selena? As important as my being first up the Monument last night?"

"I don't know." She looked away from him, let her gaze stray round the room as if each object in it were new and unknown. "No." She turned back but did not meet his eyes. "No, I guess it's not that important."

F42